"At what age," said Blaine, "did you start your travels?"

"I was ten," said Dumarest harshly. "I was alone and more than a little desperate. I stowed away on a ship and had more luck than I deserved. I have been traveling ever since."

Traveling, he thought. Going deeper and deeper into the inhabited worlds, leaping from star to star and, because stars were closest away from his home planet, moving always away from Earth. Further and further until even the legend was forgotten and the very name became a joke.

"Ten," said Blaine. "And how old are you now?"

It was a question impossible to answer.

The Dumarest of Terra Series
by E.C. Tubb, from *Ace Science Fiction:*

DERAI

E.C. TUBB

SF
ace books
A Division of Charter Communications Inc.
A GROSSET & DUNLAP COMPANY
51 Madison Avenue
New York, New York 10010

DERAI

copyright © 1968 by E.C. Tubb

An ACE Book

This Ace printing: May 1982
Published Simultaneously in Canada

2 4 6 8 0 9 7 5 3 1
Manufactured in the United States of America

Dedicated to Jennifer

I

DUMAREST was at practice when the skybeast came. He stood poised on the balls of his feet, a short bar of lead in his hand, parrying and dodging the vicious slashes and thrusts of a yard of steel. Sweat dripped from his face and naked torso; Nada wasn't playing and she was strong enough to send the steel rod whining through the turgid air. She was also sadist enough to enjoy it.

"All right," she said finally. "That's enough." She stepped back and threw aside the rod. Her blouse, taut over her breasts, was dark with perspiration. Her long, dark hair clung to her neck and cheeks. Her skin, in the dull lighting of the tent, was faintly olive. "You're fast," she said admiringly. "Fast."

"I am?" He looked down at his body. A ragged, shallow gash ran over his ribs. A deeper cut marked his left side, two others his left forearm. The wounds were almost healed beneath a layer of transparent plastic.

"You were green then," she said. "Still groggy from traveling Low. And they were lucky," she added. "Those who managed to hit you, I mean. Lucky enough to make a score but not lucky enough to win." She stepped close and stood before him. Her head came just below the level of his own. "You're good, Earl," she said. "Real good."

"I'm hot."

"Then wash." She didn't mistake his meaning. "I've put a bucket outside."

It was a five gallon drum, the top removed, almost
full of tepid water. He plunged in his arms, laving his
torso, then ducked his head. When he stood up he heard
the mournful booming. High above, drifting among the
scattered clouds, a beast was dying.

Already most of the auxiliary pods had been
punctured and hung like ragged ribbons of mist at the
edge of the great, hemispherical body. Even as he
watched, a swarm of the local skylife darted from the
clouds to tear at the intruder: rats worrying a dog. It
fought back with the fringe of tentacles hanging from
beneath its body, seizing its tormentors, sending them
plummeting with ruptured gas-sacs. Others of their
own kind ate them before they could hit the ground.
Still others continued the attack.

"It hasn't got a chance," said Nada. "Not one."
Her voice was thick with anticipation.

Abruptly the creature vomited in a desperate effort to
gain height. A cloud of water vapor and ingested food
sprayed in a kaleidoscope of colored smoke. It rose a
little, booming with terror and alarm, almost helpless
here over flat country away from the strong thermals of
its mountainous browsing grounds. High and to one
side the keepers who had driven it to the city with
air-blast and electric probe watched from the safety of
their floating platforms.

"Soon," gloated Nada. "Soon!"

The attackers darted in for the kill. They tore at the
lashing tentacles, at the soft underparts, at the tough
skin of the main gas-sac. The creature vomited again
and then, as natural hydrogen spurted from its
punctured hide, spored.

Its death-scream echoed over the city as a cloud of
glittering fragments sparkled in the air.

"Nice." Nada stared thoughtfully at the falling remnants of the creature. Around it the attackers were busy feeding. Little if any of it would reach the ground. "They're bringing in another for the finale," she said. "I was talking to the keepers. It's a real big one. They're going to burn it," she added. "At night."

Dumarest plunged his head again into the water. He rose, squeezing his hair. Droplets clung to his naked flesh like colored dew. "Do they always do that?"

"Burn one? Sure. It makes a good spectacle," she explained. "Something to give the tourists a big charge. A highlight, sort of." She smiled at her own joke. "This your first time on Kyle?"

Dumarest nodded.

"We'll be moving on soon," said the girl. "The Festival's almost over. Elgar's the next stop. Know it?"

"No."

"A lousy dump," she said dispassionately. "Then Gerath, then Segelt, then Folgone. That's a weird one," she mused. "Real weird. You coming with us?"

"No." Dumarest reached for a towel. She handed it to him.

"You could do worse," she suggested. "Aiken likes you. And," she added meaningfully, "so do I."

Dumarest busied himself with the towel.

"We'd make a fine couple," she said. "I'm all the woman you could ever use and you're all the man I'll ever want. We'd get along fine." She caught the towel he threw toward her and watched him dress. "What do you say, Earl?"

"It wouldn't work," he said. "I like to keep moving."

"Why?" she demanded. "You're looking for something," she decided. "That or you're running away from something. Which is it, Earl?"

"Neither," he said.

"Then—?"

"No," he said. And left her standing alone.

Aiken lived in a blocked-off portion at the rear of the tent, living, eating and sleeping on the premises of his concession. The proprietor was a small, round, pudgy man with a tendency to sweat. He looked up from the upended crate he used as a desk and hastily slammed the lid of a cash box. "Earl!" He twisted his face into a smile. "It's good to see you, boy. Something on your mind?"

"My share," said Dumarest. "I want it."

"Sure." Aiken began to sweat. "Your share."

"That's right." Dumarest stood to one side of the rough desk looking down at the little man. "You've had time to count it out," he said. "If you haven't I know just how much it should be. Want me to tell you?"

"No need for that," said Aiken. "I didn't think you'd be in so much of a hurry," he explained. "We've got a few days yet before the end of the Festival. How about settling up then?"

Dumarest shook his head. "Look," he said gently, "I want that money. I fought for it. I earned it. Now I want it."

"That's natural." Aiken produced a handkerchief and mopped his face and neck. "A man likes to handle the money he's earned, spend a little of it maybe. A man that's a fool, that is. But, Earl, you're no fool."

Dumarest stood, waiting.

"That money," said Aiken. "It's yours—that I'm not arguing about—but why not invest it while you've got the chance? Listen," he urged. "This is a nice little setup. We've got Nada as a flash to con in the goops. A couple of steadies who bleed fast and a comic who's good for a laugh. With you in the ring we can't lose. We can offer odds of ten-to-one on first blood and still clean up. Better yet, we can take on the private fights. You know, ten inch knives and no quarter. Big money, Earl. Big money."

"No," said Dumarest.

"You're letting slip the chance of a lifetime."

"Maybe. Where's my share?"

"You seen Nada? She wants to talk to you."

"I've seen her." Dumarest leaned forward, his face hard. "What's the matter, Aiken? Don't you want to pay me?"

"Sure I do," said the proprietor. His eyes were darting, furtive. "Sure I do," he repeated, "only—" He broke off, swallowing. "Look, Earl," he said desperately. "I'll give it to you straight. Things haven't been going so good. The concession cost more than I figured and the goops have been staying away. What I'm trying to say is that I'm practically broke. I owe the others. I've got to find freight and passage money to the next stop on the circuit. There are bills due in town. With your share I can just about make it."

"And without?"

"I'm beaten," admitted Aiken. "I'll be stranded. Finished."

"Too bad," said Dumarest. "Pay me."

"But—"

Dumarest reached out and caught the other man by the shoulder. Gently he tightened his fingers. "I worked for that money," he said quietly. "I chanced getting myself killed to earn it. Now do you give it to me or do I help myself?"

Outside the tent he counted the money. It was barely enough for a single High passage on a ship that wasn't traveling too far. Thoughtfully he walked down the midway section of the carnival. Concessions stood to either side, some open, most waiting for night, when the square mile set aside for the Festival games really came to life. An amplified voice yelled to him from a tent:

"Hey, you there! Want to know what it's like to be burned to death? Full-sense feelies give the thrill of a lifetime! Genuine recordings of impalement, live-burial, flaying, dismemberment and many more. Sixteen different types of torture! You feel it, sense it, know what it's like. Hurry! Hurry! Hurry!"

The male voice fell silent. A female voice whispered from lower down the line:

"Hello, handsome! Want to share my wedding night? Find out just how the little woman feels. Adapt your technique. Get the reputation of a man who knows what it's all about. Please the ladies. Step right up for a new experience!"

A third voice, quieter, without amplification: "Alms, brother?"

A monk of the Universal Brotherhood stood by the gate in the perimeter fence. He had a pale, thin face framed by the cowl of his homespun robe. He held out his chipped plastic begging bowl as Dumarest halted. "Of your charity, brother," he said. "Remember the poor."

"How could I forget them?" Dumarest threw coins into the bowl. "How could anyone? You have much work on Kyle, Brother."

"You speak truth," said the monk. He looked at the coins in his bowl. Dumarest had been generous. "Your name, brother?"

"So that I shall be mentioned in your prayers?"

Dumarest smiled but gave the information. The monk stepped closer.

"There is a man who seeks you," he said quietly. "A man of influence and power. It would be to your advantage to attend him."

"Thank you, Brother." The monks, Dumarest knew, had friends in high places and an information network that spread across the galaxy. The Universal Brotherhood, for all the humbleness, was a very real power. "His name?"

"Moto Shamaski. A factor in the city. You will attend?"

"Yes," said Dumarest. "Keep well, Brother."

"Keep well."

The factor had gray hair, gray eyes, a gray beard shaved in the pattern of his Guild. His skin was a faded saffron, creped with wrinkles, pouched beneath slanting eyes. He rose as Dumarest entered the office and inclined his head in greeting. "You have not kept me waiting," he said. His voice was thin, precise. "It is appreciated. You will accept refreshment?"

"Thank you, no." Dumarest glanced around the office before taking the proffered chair. It was a soft, luxurious place, the carpet thick underfoot, the ceiling a mesh of sound-trapping fiber. A few simple designs ornamented the paneled walls, delicate embroideries of intricate construction, rare and valuable examples of Sha' Tung art. Moto Shamaski was a rich and cultured man.

"It is good of you to attend me," he said. "I trust that you have suffered no inconvenience?"

"None." Dumarest wasn't deluded as to his own importance: men such as the factor were always polite.

"I received word that you wanted to see me," he said.
"Apparently you do. May I ask why?"

The factor smiled with his lips, not his eyes—they
were busy searching the visitor. Dumarest recognized
the ritual: let the silence grow and it would, perhaps,
reveal something of interest, impatience, arrogance,
servility or simply an overriding need to talk.

Impassively he leaned back, letting his eyes drift
from the factor to where a sheet of unbroken crystal
occupied the major part of one wall. It gave a clear view
of the sky and the famous Clouds of Kyle.

"Beautiful, are they not?" The factor leaned forward, looking at the colored shadows brushing the face
of his visitor. It was a strong face, hard, determined.
The face of a man who learned to live without the
protection of Guild, House or Organization. "I have
been thirty years on Kyle," he said quietly. "Never do
I tire of watching the sky."

Dumarest made no comment.

"Such tiny organisms to create such splendor,"
mused the factor. "Living, breeding, dying in their
great swarms high above the ground. Food for others
who share their aerial environment. A thing unique to
Kyle and for which the planet has cause to be grateful."

"The Festival," said Dumarest. He turned from the
window to face the man across the desk. "The time
when the skybeasts turn from their browsing to fight in
the fury of mating. That," he said dryly, "and other
things."

It was the factor's turn to make no comment.
Shamaski was an old man, a lover of beauty who
preferred not to dwell on the other aspects of the Festival, the games and wild lusts, the perversions and
pandering to bestiality which wiled away the long
nights for the impatient tourists who brought their

wealth to Kyle. Instead he gestured toward a tray standing on a small table to one side of the room. "Are you sure that you require nothing? Some tea, perhaps?"

Dumarest shook his head, his eyes thoughtful. The man had sent for him; why did he delay?

"You are. impatient," said the factor shrewdly. "And, no doubt, a little curious. They are natural attributes but you mask them well." He pressed a button at the edge of his desk. A panel glowed on the flat surface, the brightness marked with lines of script. "Earl Dumarest," read Shamaski. "A traveler. You arrived here from Gleece traveling Low. Before Gleece you were on Pren, before that on Exon, Aime, Stulgar. Before Stulgar you were the guest of the Matriarch of Kund. You traveled with her retinue from Gath where, I assume, you were able to be of some service." He looked up from the desk. "Is the information correct?"

"It is," said Dumarest. He wondered at the factor's resources to have been able to learn so much in so short a time. The monks, perhaps? Or could he be the subject of disseminated news? The thought was disturbing.

"On arrival here," continued the factor, "you entered into an arrangement with a concessionaire specializing in the staging of hand-combats. You have had moderate success. However, the Festival is almost over and further opportunities for making money are limited. Again, do you agree?" he darkened the panel at Dumarest's nod. "You are shrewd, capable and experienced," summed up the factor. "Young enough to be resourceful and old enough to be discreet. A happy combination."

"You want to employ me," said Dumarest abruptly.

The factor agreed. "Would you accept a commission from my hands?"

"It depends," said Dumarest, "on just what it is."

The factor rose, crossed to the tray, returned bearing
cups of scented tea. "It is really quite simple," he
explained. "I want you to escort a young person to
Hive. You know it?"

Dumarest was cautious. "No."

"A remote world some distance from here and rela-
tively unimportant. The planet is managed by a syndi-
cate of Houses and the person you are to escort is a
member of one of them." The factor sipped, savoring
his tea. "Such houses," he hinted, "are not ungener-
ous."

"Perhaps not," said Dumarest. "But is it ever wise
to trust to the gratitude of princes?"

"No," admitted Shamaski. He sipped more tea. "I
will give you the cost of three High passages. You
accept?"

Dumarest hesitated. "You say that Hive is a remote
world," he pointed out. "I will probably have to wait
for a ship and then I will have to pay my passage. How
am I expected to make a profit?"

"You did not intend going to Hive?"

"No," lied Dumarest.

"Very well," decided the factor. "I will give you
the cost of two High passages. Clear," he added. "I
shall pay the expenses of the outward journey. Is that
satisfactory?"

Dumarest slowly finished his tea and set down the
cup. The factor had been a little too eager to raise his
offer. Idly he dipped a finger in the dregs and ran it
around the edge. A thin, high ringing filled the office, a
note of absolute purity. "A question," he said, lifting
his finger. "You say that this person is a member of an
established House. Why do they not send an escort of
their own?"

The factor was patient. "It is a question of time. It is

quicker to send the person concerned than to send a message and wait for an escort.''

It was true enough but the answer was revealing. The person, then, was of some importance. Dumarest probed a little deeper. "There is need for haste?''

"There is no reason for delay,'' said the factor. He was, Dumarest guessed, becoming a little irritated. "Soon the ships will be leaving Kyle. Delay now may necessitate special charter. Will you take the commission? Subject, of course, to your being accepted by the person concerned. That,'' he added, "is an essential part of the contract.''

"Naturally.'' Dumarest made up his mind. He had pressed the factor as far as he would go—more and he would lose the opportunity. "I accept,'' he said. "When do I meet my charge?''

"At once.'' Shamaski pressed a button and a panel slid open in the wall. "Permit me to introduce the Lady Derai of the House of Caldor. My lady, this is Earl Dumarest, who, with your permission, will be your guide and protector.'' He extended his hand to help her step into the office.

She was tall, as slender as a reed, with hair so silver it was almost colorless. *A child, thought Dumarest. A scared and frightened child.* Then he saw her eyes, enormous in the bone-white pallor of her face. Not a child, he corrected himself. A young woman, nubile at least, but still scared, still afraid. But of what?

"My lady.'' He stood, very tall, as the factor left her side.

"You look surprised,'' said Shamaski softly. "I cannot blame you.'' He moved toward the tray, poured tea, spoke quietly across the cup. "She came to me a few weeks ago in an extreme state of shock and panic. A monk had found her down at the landing field. I took

her under my protection. I am a factor," he explained.
"A man of business. Her House has power and is not
without influence. I have had dealings with them in the
past and hope to have more in the future. The Brother
knew of my interest and she sought my aid."

"Why?"

"She trusted me. I was the only one she felt she could
trust."

"I didn't mean that," said Dumarest impatiently.
"Why did she seek your aid? For what?"

"For sanctuary. For somewhere safe to rest. For
protection."

"The member of an established House?" Dumarest
frowned; the thing was illogical. Surely she would have
traveled with her own retinue? "It doesn't make
sense," he pointed out. "Why didn't she appeal to
those of her own kind? What was she doing here anyway?"

"She had run away," said the factor. "She took
passage on the first available ship and it brought her
here to Kyle. She arrived at the commencement of the
Festival," he added bitterly. "With the streets
thronged with perverted beasts hoping to see beauty
destroyed and the skies filled with death. Those who
attend the games and who pay for the sight of blood.
You should know them."

"They are men," said Dumarest. "And women.
Bored, hungry for new sensations, eager for excitement. People on holiday. Are they to be blamed if Kyle
is willing to cater to their basest needs?"

"Who is really to blame?" mused the factor. "The
pervert, or those who pander to his perversion? The
question has been pondered since men first discovered
ethics. There has yet to be found a satisfying answer."

"Perhaps there never will." Dumarest turned as the

girl moved toward them, admiring the way she walked, her feet seeming to glide over the carpet. Her hair was so fine it lifted with the wind of her passage. "My lady?"

"When do we leave?" she asked. "Will it be soon?"

"You accept me as your escort, my lady?"

"I accept. When do we leave?"

Her voice was warm, rich, in sharp contrast to her bloodless lips. *Anemia,* thought Dumarest dispassionately, *or leukemia, but why was she suffering from such minor ills if she had the wealth of a House to summon medical aid?* He looked at her, more sharply than before. She was too thin for her height. Her eyes were too large, her neck too long, her hands too delicate. Framed by the silver cascade of her hair her face had a peculiar, unfinished appearance, as if she had sprung too early from the womb. And yet she was beautiful.

"It will be soon, my lady," promised Shamaski. "As soon as can be arranged."

She nodded and drifted away to toy absently with the edges of the desk.

Dumarest watched her as he spoke to the factor. "There is something I don't understand," he said softly. "You want me to take her to Hive. She obviously wants to go there. Why?"

"It is her home."

"And yet she ran away?"

"I did not say that she had run from Hive," reminded the factor.

"True." Dumarest had taken too much for granted. "But why can't she travel alone? She did it once, why not again?"

"She is afraid," said Shamaski. "Surely you can sense that? And yet her fear is nothing to what it was. When she came to me she was terrified. Never before have I seen a human in such fear."

He must, thought Dumarest, *have had wide experience of the emotion. Especially on Kyle during the Festival.* "All right," he said. "So she is afraid to travel alone. That I can understand. But why did she run away?"

"The same reason. Fear."

"Fear of what?"

"Of her life. She was convinced that someone intended to kill her. She could think of nothing but the necessity of flight. You can understand now," said the factor, "why it is essential that she should trust her escort. She will travel with no other."

A paranoiac, thought Dumarest bleakly. *So that's what all this is about: The girl is insane.* He felt pity but not surprise. Old families tended to inbreed to the point where harmful genes became predominant, and great Houses were the worst offenders. But why hadn't they treated her? Why, at least, hadn't they cauterized that portion of the brain governing fear?

He dismissed the question. It was no concern of his. For the cost of two High passages he was willing to do more than just escort a mentally unstable girl to her home world. Especially when that world was somewhere he wanted to reach.

"Please," she said again, looking up. "We will leave soon?"

"Yes, my lady," said Dumarest. "Soon."

II

DUMAREST booked passage on a small ship carrying mixed cargo and passengers to Hive. It wasn't the best of its kind but it was the first to leave and he was in a hurry to get moving. It would be a long journey. Not for those traveling Low, riding doped, frozen and ninety percent dead in the bleak, cold-region of the ship, resting in boxes designed to hold livestock. For them the journey would take no time at all. For some it would be the last journey they would ever make, the unlucky fifteen percent who had chanced their luck once too often and who would never awake.

Nor for those traveling High. They enjoyed the magic of quick-time, the drug slowing their metabolism so that time streamed past and a day seemed less than an hour. Even for them, though, time existed and had to be killed in traditional ways.

"Five." A thin man with hollowed cheeks and furtive eyes pushed a small stack of coins to the center of the table. Reflected light gleamed from the heavy ring he wore on one finger. "And raise five more."

A fat man, a free-lance trader, looked at his cards and pursed his lips. "I'll stay."

Two others followed his example, quiet men wearing expensive clothing, representatives of commercial empires. The fifth man shook his head and discarded his hand. The sixth, another trader, hesitated, then decided to remain in the game. Dumarest sat, watching.

"That man," whispered the girl at his side. "The one with the ring. He's cheating."

"Are you sure, my lady?" Like the girl Dumarest kept his voice low. He found the accusation amusing. It was very probable that the gambler would cheat given the opportunity, but it was most unlikely the girl would know of it.

"I'm sure," she insisted. "He will win this hand. You'll see."

The gambler won.

Luck, thought Dumarest. *She's probably heard that all ships are staffed with professional gamblers waiting to fleece the unwary. Well, on a ship like this that could be true enough, but even an honest gambler had to win at times.*

"He cheated," she said. "I think you know it. Is that why you're not playing?"

Dumarest shook his head. Normally he would have joined in the game but gambling demanded concentration and the girl was his first responsibility. He looked at her where she sat. She had lost her aura of fear and the loss had improved her. *Like a child on a treat*, he thought. *A girl on a holiday. It's a pity she's so thin.*

The thought was the prelude to action. He looked around the lounge. It was lit by a central light, cluttered with chairs, the table occupying most of the free space. To one side spigots protruded from a wall with a rack of cups beneath. He rose, crossed to them, filled two of the cups with a creamy liquid. Returning, he offered one to the girl.

"What is it?" She looked suspiciously at the container.

"Food, my lady. It is wise that you should eat."

"I'm not hungry."

"Even so, my lady, it is best to eat." *While you have*

the chance, he thought grimly. Anyway, it was all included in the fare.

Sitting, he took a swallow of the thick liquid. It was Basic, thick with protein, cloying with glucose, laced with vitamins. A cupful provided a spaceman with a day's basic ration of food. He sipped again. The liquid was at blood-heat, kept that way by the mechanism in the base of the container.

"I don't like this," complained the girl. "I want something solid."

On a larger ship she could have had it. Cold, of course, since no solid food could retain its heat during the long quick-time journey from plate to mouth. But this wasn't a large ship and they had to take what was offered.

"Eat my lady," he said curtly. *Didn't she realize the importance of food?* "Eat," he said again, his tone more gentle. "It will do you good."

She obeyed, mechanically, her eyes wide as they stared at the players over the rim of the cup. "He's going to win again," she said. "The one with the ring."

Dumarest looked toward the table. The players were at the draw, the gambler about to deal. "Two," said the fat trader. The gambler dealt two cards facedown and pushed them across the table. "Three," said the first representative. "One," said his companion. The other two players had dropped out.

"He will give himself three cards," whispered the girl. "And he will win."

The gambler won.

"How did you know, my lady?" Dumarest had watched but had seen nothing suspicious.

"I just knew." She put aside the empty cup. "Must you call me that?"

"My lady?"

"That's what I mean. My name is Derai. Yours is Earl. Must we be so formal?"

"As you wish." It was a small thing; they would part at the end of the journey. At the moment there was something of greater importance. "Derai, are you a clairvoyant?"

"I cannot read the future."

"Then how did you know the gambler would give himself three cards and win?"

She turned, not answering, the cascade of silver hiding her face. Dumarest wondered at her sudden sensitivity. Then she faced him again, her eyes bright with excitement. "Would you like to play, Earl? I could tell you how to win."

"Perhaps," he said dryly. "But the others might object."

"Does it matter? You need money and this is a chance to get it. Why do you refuse?"

He sighed, wondering how to explain.

"Never mind," she decided. "I shall play myself. Will you please lend me some money?" Then, as he hesitated, "I will pay you back with profit from my winnings."

"And if you lose?"

"You must trust me," she said seriously. "I shall not lose."

The cabin was small, dimly lit, giving privacy and very little else. It held two opposed bunks and one of them glittered with coins. Derai had flung them there. She had, Dumarest remembered, practically cleaned the others out. He still couldn't understand how she had done it.

"What did I tell you?" She lay on the other bunk,

hardly denting the pneumatic mattress, her hair spread wide on the pillow. The dim light gave color to her face, enhanced the brightness of her eyes. "Take it," she urged. "All of it. It's yours."

Dumarest gathered up the coins and knew that some of them were metaphorical blood. The others had been philosophical about their losses, but not the gambler. He had grown desperate, the hollow cheeks tight against the bones of his skull, the sweat beading his forehead each time he lost a hand. Dumarest could guess why. His losses had been too heavy. His debts were possibly large. If he rode on a delayed-payment basis, a common practice of his kind, the captain would have the right to bond him to servitude unless he could pay. And Dumarest guessed that he couldn't pay. Not now. Such a man could be dangerous. It was possible that he would seek revenge.

"Earl!" said Derai. "Earl!"

He turned. The girl was panting, her eyes wide with terror, thin hands clutched in the region of her heart. He knelt, ignoring the too-sudden shock of impact as his knees hit the deck, his fingers gentle on her wrist. Her pulse was racing. He didn't have to ask what was wrong. He could sense it, the aura of fear which enfolded her like a living thing. But why? He looked around; the cabin was empty of any threat.

"Earl!"

"I'm here," he soothed. "You don't have to worry." He forced conviction into his voice. "Do you really believe that I would ever allow anything to harm you?" He felt a sudden wave of protective tenderness. She was too young, too delicate to have to carry such an emotional burden. He felt her fingers slip into his own.

"That man," she said. "The one with the ring. Do you think he hates me?"

"Probably." He agreed. "But he doesn't really mean it. He's just angry because you won all his money. Angry and a little desperate. Afraid too," he added. "More afraid than you and with better reason." *Which*, he thought dully, *wasn't really true. No one could be more afraid than a paranoiac because they knew, without any question of doubt, that the entire universe was against them.* "I'll take care of the gambler," he decided. "I'll give him back his money. That will stop him from hating you."

"You're a good man, Earl."

"I'm a fool," he said. "He doesn't deserve it. But I'll do it to make you happy." He rose and paused by the door. "I'll lock you in," he said. "Don't open the door to anyone. Promise?" She nodded. "Settle down now," he advised. "Try to get some sleep."

"You'll be back?"

"I'll be back."

Outside the cabin he hesitated, wondering just where the gambler was to be found. There was only one logical place; the man couldn't afford to rest or sleep. He heard the sound of angry voices as he approached the lounge.

"You dirty cheat!" The fat trader had the gambler by the throat. "I saw you switch that card. I've a mind to tear out your eyes!"

"Tearing out his fingers would be a better bet," suggested the other trader. "That'll teach him a lesson."

The three of them were alone in the lounge; the others had retired. Dumarest stepped forward and looked at the gambler. The fat man was supporting the gambler's weight, the flesh white around his knuckles.

"Take it easy," said Dumarest. "Your arm," he explained as the fat trader glared at him. "How long do

you think you could support that load in normal circumstances?''

The fat man released the gambler and stood rubbing
his arm. ''I forgot,'' he said sheepishly. ''I must have
been holding him up for close to half a day, objective
time. Thanks for reminding me.''

''Forget it. Was he cheating?''

''Like an amateur,'' said the other trader. ''He must
have thought we were blind.''

''Got your money back? All right,'' said Dumarest
as they nodded, ''I guess you're all through with him
now.'' He reached out and took the gambler by the
upper arm. ''Let's take a walk,'' he suggested. ''A
short stroll down to your cabin.'' He closed his fingers
until he felt bone. ''Move!''

It was a cramped place, dingy, the bottom of the
heap. The lowest member of the crew had better ac-
commodations and certainly more self-respect.
Dumarest threw the gambler toward the bunk and
leaned back against the door. ''You've hit the bottom,''
he said casually. ''You're broke, in debt and scared of
what's going to happen. Right?''

The man nodded, massaging his throat. ''That's
right,'' he said painfully. ''You come to gloat?''

''No. What's your name?''

''Eldon. Sar Eldon. Why? What do you want?''

''I'm running an errand.'' Coins showered to the
bunk from Dumarest's hand. The cost of a High passage plus five percent. ''The girl you played with and
who won your money. She's sending it back.''

Eldon stared unbelievingly at the coins.

''How did she win it?'' asked Dumarest. ''Don't tell
me it was luck,'' he added. ''I know better. Luck had
nothing to do with it.''

''I don't know.'' The gambler's hands trembled as

he collected the money. "I had a stacked deck," he admitted. "I knew just which cards to take so as to wind up with the winning hand. Usually I can manage a game but not this time. Everything went wrong. She kept taking the wrong number of cards and ruining my draw. I was outsmarted all along the line. Who is she?"

"It doesn't matter." Dumarest opened the door and looked back. "Take some advice, Sar. Quit this ship while you've got the chance. If you want to know why take a look at where they keep you. And don't think those traders won't complain."

"I'll quit," said Eldon. "And thanks. See you on Hive?"

"Maybe," said Dumarest.

Back in the lounge the traders were talking. Dumarest drew himself another cup of Basic. He didn't particularly like the stuff but he had traveled Low too often not to appreciate its value. And any traveler, if he had sense, ate when he could. Food was as important as a good pair of boots. As he sipped he listened; much could be learned from idle talk. From listening he joined the conversation and then, when it was appropriate, slipped in a question of his own.

"Earth?" The fat trader blinked his surprise. "That's a queer name. You might as well call a planet soil or dirt or ground. Every planet's got earth. They grow things in it. Earth!"

"It's a legend," said his companion.

"You've heard of it?" One day, thought Dumarest, he had to be lucky. Someone, somewhere, would be able to tell him what he wanted to know. This man?

"No, but I've heard of others. Jackpot, El Dorado, Bonanza. All legends. Land on any world and you'll get a load of them. Why, you won't believe this, but I've even heard of a man who claims that we all originated on one world. Crazy, of course.''

"He'd have to be," said the fat trader. "How could all of mankind come from one world? It stands to reason that it just isn't possible. Legends," he said, shaking his head. "Who wants legends?" He looked at Dumarest. "Care to sit in on a game?"

"No thanks," said Dumarest. "I'm a little tired. Later, maybe."

Derai was awake when he returned to the cabin. She sat propped high on the pillow, the silver of her hair a dull sheen in the shadowed lighting. She gestured for him to approach. "You gave him the money? He was pleased?"

"Yes, my lady."

"Derai—I do not want to have to tell you again." She was imperious with unconscious arrogance. "Sit beside me," she ordered. "I need your protection."

"Protection?" The cabin was empty, silent aside from the faint, almost inaudible vibration of the Erhaft drive. "From what?"

"From myself, perhaps." She closed her eyes and he could sense her fatigue, the chronic tiredness that must be a part of her condition. Paranoia and insomnia went hand in hand. "Talk to me," she demanded. "Tell me of yourself. You have traveled much?"

"I have."

"But never before to Hive?"

"No."

"But you want to go there." She opened her eyes and stared into his own. "You want to go there?"

Dumarest nodded, not speaking, studying her face in the dim glow of the light. Again she had changed. The

childishness had vanished, the diffidence, the aura of
fear. So much he had already seen. But now her eyes
held maturity and a strange intensity.

"I have been lying here," she said, "thinking. Of
myself and of you and the working of fate. I have come
to a conclusion."

Dumarest waited, held by the almost hypnotic intensity of her eyes.

"I want you," she said abruptly. "I need you. When
you are close I feel safe and protected. I think, if you
would stay, I could even sleep. It has been a long time
since I really slept," she whispered. "Longer still that I
have been able to rest without dreams. You will stay?"

"If you wish." Dumarest could see no harm. He
would rather not but, if it would comfort her, he would
stay.

"I need you," she repeated. "You must never leave
me."

Words, he thought. *A child playing at being a woman
and not knowing what she is saying*, and then he remembered the expression he had seen in her eyes. No
child could look like that. No young, innocent girl,
even though nubile. She had worn the expression of an
experienced woman who knew what she wanted and
was determined to get it. He felt her hand slip into his
own.

"You are afraid," she murmured. "Why?" And
then, before he could answer, "You are wrong. I am no
spoiled bitch seeking pleasure. No highborn lady demanding attention and not realizing that it is given
through fear and not affection. I am not playing with
you, Earl. You don't have to be afraid. A place will be
found for you. My House is tolerant. I am bespoken to
no suitor. There is no bar to our union." Her hand
closed on his own. "We shall be very happy."

It was, he thought, *one of the strangest proposals there ever could have been.* Strange and ludicrous. Pathetic and potentially dangerous. *She's insane,* he reminded himself. Living in a world of nightmare and refusing to accept reality. Or, if not refusing, totally unable. No House could be as tolerant as she claimed. Their answer to what she proposed would be to send for an assassin.

"No," she whispered. "You are wrong. I would never let that happen."

How could she stop it?

"I would stop it," she said. "You must trust me, Earl. Always you must trust me."

She was, he realized, almost asleep, barely conscious of what she was saying. Gently he tried to remove his hand but her grip was too tight.

"You are a strange man," she murmured. "I have never met anyone like you before. With you I could be a real woman—you have strength enough for us both. So strong," she whispered. "So indifferent to danger. It must be wonderful not to live in fear."

Carefully he eased himself into a more comfortable position. Soon she would be asleep. Then, perhaps, he would be able to leave.

"No! You must not go! You must never leave me!" Her hand closed with spasmodic force. "I have much to give you," she said, calmer now. "I can help you in so many ways. I can tell you about Earth."

"Earth?" He leaned forward, staring at the closed lids of her eyes, willing her to answer. "What do you know about Earth?"

"A bleak place," she said. "Scarred by ancient wars. And yet it holds a strange kind of life."

"Yes?" He was impatient in his eagerness. "What else?"

"You want to find it," she said. "You want to find it very much. For you it is home." Her voice sank to a fading whisper. Then, very softly, just before she yielded to sleep: "I love you, Earl. And you are wrong about me. So very wrong. I am not insane."

No, he thought bleakly, *you're not insane. Not in the way I'd imagined, at least, but you think you're in love with me and you've betrayed yourself.*

She had done it earlier, of course, but then he had been only mildly suspicious. Now he knew beyond any question of doubt. No wonder Shamaski had been so eager to get rid of her. No wonder she had won so easily at cards. And Earth? He swallowed his bitterness. He knew now how she had known about that. Known it and tried to trap him with the knowledge, offering it as a tempting bait.

He looked at her hand, so small and delicate within his own. He looked at her long, slender lines, the incredible softness of her hair, her ethereal grace. He felt again the sudden wave of protective tenderness.

A defense mechanism, he told himself. *An amusement of the glands. A biological reaction triggered by cortical stimulation. Or*, he wondered, *was it simple pity?* It was easy to pity someone so frail and lovely. Easier still knowing what she was. But pity was dangerously close to love. Too close.

He looked away, staring at the cabin door, the hard, unemotional wall, the bare symmetry of the spartan furnishings. Anywhere but at the beautiful woman at his side. The Lady Derai of the House of Caldor. His charge . . .

Derai . . . who was a natural-born telepath.

III

THE LIBRARY was a big place, long, broad, high enough for a gallery with huge fireplaces at either end. Once it had been the great hall of the stronghold but, as the House had grown, so had the building; now the fireplaces were blocked, the windows filled, the walls lined with books and records instead of banners, trophies and weapons.

Only the blazons on the chimney breasts remained unchanged: the Caldor insignia deep-cut into imperishable stone, a hand, grasping.

It would be grasping, thought Blaine with cynical amusement. The Caldors were noted for their greed but then, he admitted, so were the Fentons, the Tomblains, the Egreths and all the rest of the eleven Houses which now ruled Hive.

Once it had been twenty-three, but that had been before the Pact had fraozen the status quo. Now it was eleven. Soon, inevitably, it would be less. He wondered if Caldor would be among those to survive.

He turned and looked down the library. It was dimly lit by modified flambeaux but, at a table toward the center of the room, a man sat in a wash of light. It came from the viewer at which he worked, throwing his face into sharp relief. Sergal, the librarian, was as old and dusty as his cherished books. Blaine moved toward him, soft-footed on the stone-paved floor, coming up from behind so that he could look at the viewer over the old man's shoulder. He frowned at what he saw. "What are you doing?"

"My lord!" Sergal started, almost falling from his chair. "My lord, I did not hear you. I—"

"Relax." Blaine felt a momentary guilt at having startled the old man. And Sergal was old, older than his father and almost as old as grandfather, who was so old that he was more dead than alive. He leaned forward, studying the viewer. It showed a portion of the family tree, not just the record of births, deaths and unions, but in more exact detail; the genetic patterns displayed in a color-code of dots and lines, the history of genes and chromosomes. "For Uncle Emil?"

"Not exactly, my lord." Sergal was uneasy. "He gave full authority," he hastened to add, "but I'm copying this data for the cyber."

"Regor?" Blaine shrugged. The cyber was more robot than human and probably had some intellectual curiosity regarding the ancient records. Idly he operated the viewer, later data flashing on the screen, halting as he found what he wanted. His own record of birth, marred, as he had known it would be, by the sinister black mark of bastardy. Impatiently he restored the instrument to its original setting. "I thought that Emil would have had you hard at work," he said, "checking the old records which might be of use. Pre-Pact stuff," he explained. "Something which he could claim carried a prior right."

"The Pact abrogates any and all prior commitments, my lord," said Sergal stiffly. "Article Twelve is very specific on the matter."

"I know," said Blaine. "But you couldn't blame him for trying. Did he try?"

"Yes, my lord."

He would, thought Blaine. Emil wouldn't leave a

thing undone if he suspected that it could give him an advantage. But checking the old records was an act of desperation—the Pact could not so easily be broken. *Or,* he wondered, *could it be that Emil was merely throwing down a smoke-screen? Searching wildly for something he knew he couldn't find in order to cover something else?*

Thoughtfully Blaine moved over to the side of the room. Here were stacked the old, dusty, crumbling volumes of a bygone age. He opened one at random and read a list of names. He flipped a few pages and tried again.

The Sorgasson Incident, he read. *At the base of the Weeping Mountain the Houses of Caldor and Sorgasson met in combat to decide the harvesting rights of the region running from the base of the mountain to the sea; from the Cal river to the Sorg crevass. The House of Caldor was victorious. The undermentioned died in glory for the honor of Caldor.*

And their reward, thought Blaine, is to be noted in the rotting pages of a book no one bothers to read. So much for glory. He closed the book and replaced it on the shelf, wondering a little about the old days when men marched to war wearing armor, perhaps bearing weapons of edged steel, and carrying banners.

The details were in the books, of course, as the types of weapons would be stored in the upper gallery, no longer on display, but still available in case of need. Caldor was known for its frugality.

The click of the viewer reminded him of Sergal. The librarian added another photocopy to the growing heap at his side. His hands trembled as he worked, something Blaine had never noticed before. As he watched, the librarian fumbled a setting and looked blankly at a ruined copy.

"Let me help you." Blaine eased the old man from the chair and took his place. The data on the viewer was almost up to date; his own birth stood out with its black mark. He looked at another. Derai, his half-sister, seven years younger than himself. She had no black mark but a red splotch, almost as bad. Their father had married her mother against the wishes of the House.

He had guts that time, thought Blaine. *He defied the Old Man and went ahead regardless, and so Derai's legitimate and I'm not. It makes a difference,* he mused. *I'm with the House but not of it, but her position is established. That's luck.*

He wasn't resentful or envious. They got on well and shared one thing in common: the same father. Two things really, since neither had a living mother. His own was a nameless someone who had loved not wisely but too well. Derai's was almost equally as unknown. They had her name, her genetic pattern, but that was all. She had come from no established House.

He took the copy, his untrained fingers spoiling the setting so that the fine detail was blurred. Philosophically he tried again, pausing to frown at a scrap of data. *Ustar,* he thought. *Trust him to make a botch of things.* His cousin, younger than himself but older than Derai, the only child of his uncle Emil. Emil, who was the second son of the Old Man.

Carefully Blaine took the copy, this time perfectly. *Fate,* he thought. *Had mother married Father I'd have been in the direct line of succession. That's why Emil was so adamant that I should not be officially recognized. Then he managed to sire Ustar. Then Father married and sired Derai. Fate,* he repeated to himself. *That's all it is.*

He finished taking the series of copies. Sergal muttered his thanks. "Your uncle is waiting for them," he said. "I assume he will give them to the cyber. I'd better take them up right away."

"I shouldn't," said Blaine. "He's with a trader."

Sergal looked nonplussed.

"I'll take them," decided Blaine. "I'll pass them over when it's convenient. Leave it to me."

"As you wish, my lord."

Blaine nodded, scooping up the papers, his manner absent. Seeing the records had reminded him of something he had almost forgotten and he felt the skin crawl a little between his shoulders. When young he'd often cursed his father for not having married his mother. Now he was rather glad that he hadn't. Had Blaine been legitimate the chances were high that, by now, he would have been dead.

Scuto Dakarti was a smooth man, well-fed, well-spoken, excellently dressed. He had a fondness for jewels and expensive perfume, both of which he wore with restraint. He was also a very cautious man. "I had hoped to see the Head of the House, my lord," he said deferentially. "With respect—are you he?"

"I am the acting Head," said Emil Caldor. "My father is very old. He cannot be disturbed for items of minor importance."

"You then are Johan Caldor?"

"That is my brother. I am Emil."

"But not the eldest, my lord?" The trader had done his homework. "You will pardon my caution but the nature of my business is so delicate that I would not like to reveal it to the wrong person. A matter of confidence, you understand."

Emil looked closer at the trader. There was steel beneath the fat, a cunning brain behind the polite smile. The man had the air of a conspirator. "Who sent you?" he asked abruptly.

"A friend, my lord. A mutual acquaintance. Need I say more?"

As yet he had said nothing. Emil leaned back in his chair and slowly helped himself to wine. The goblet filled, he replaced the decanter; then, as if at an afterthought, gestured his visitor to the tray. "If you are thirsty help yourself."

"Thank you, my lord." The trader masked his feelings well. "An excellent vintage," he murmured after having poured and swallowed. "The wines of Caldor are famed over many planets."

"Did you come to bargain for wine?"

"No, my lord."

A muscle jumped high on Emil's cheek. Setting down the goblet he rose and paced the narrow confines of the room. The trader had been shown into an antechamber high in a tower. The furnishings were sparse, the walls thick, the possibility of eavesdropping remote. From a narrow window he looked down to where the trader's flitter stood in the central square.

Turning, he stared down at the man. "Very well," he said coldly. "Since you force me to ask: Why are you here?"

Deliberately the man finished his wine. He felt in full control of the situation. Leaning back he looked at his host. *Tall*, he thought, *thin, burning himself out with nervous energy. Old too, but real age is impossible to tell among the rulers of Hive. They all look so much younger. But he's interested. He hasn't thrown me out. It looks as if my guess was right.*

"My lord," he said carefully, "before I speak have I your word that I shall be permitted to leave unharmed?"

"You are beginning to intrigue me," said Emil. He resumed his seat. "Yes, you have my word."

The trader nodded as if with relief. "Thank you, my lord." He paused, thinking, then went on. "Hive is a small world. It sells honey, wax, perfume and a hundred flavors of liqueur, wine and spirit all with a honey base. But many planets produce similar goods. The real wealth of Hive does not rest with those things."

Emil raised his eyebrows. "No?"

"The real wealth of Hive lies in something else," said the trader quickly. "In the jelly, my lord. The royal jelly."

"You are talking of ambrosaira," said Emil. "It is no secret."

"But it is a thing which is not advertised," said the trader. "My lord, I will put it to you plainly. I am interested in buying ambrosaira."

Emil leaned back, a little disappointed, a little annoyed. "Why come to me about this? You must surely know of the procedure. All ambrosaira for sale is offered at auction. You are free to bid."

"Admitted, my lord. But the lots comprise little of what I want with much of what I do not. I would like to buy direct."

"Impossible!"

"Is it, my lord?"

Emil stared at the man; had there been a hint in his voice? But surely he must know of the Pact, or at least that part of it which applied to trading.

"I know, my lord," said Scuto when asked the question. "What manner of trader would I be if I did not? All produce is pooled. All is made into lots and each lot includes a little or more of ambrosaira. The lots are sold at auction. All monies received are divided equally between the ruling Houses." The trader looked up at the ceiling. It was of vault stone. "A good system, my lord, or so it would seem. I doubt if you would agree.''

"Why me?''

"You are an ambitious man, my lord.'' Now the trader looked directly into Emil's eyes. "Such a system leaves no room for ambition. All share equally—so why should one work harder than the rest? I asked myself that question, my lord, and thought of an answer. Suppose an ambitious man was to work a little harder than normal. He would collect more ambrosaira. He would not add it to the general store but would keep it by in a safe place. One day, he would think, it would be possible to sell it direct and thus gain all of the profit. If there was such a man, my lord,'' said the trader carefully, "he would have need of a man such as myself.''

"To handle the deal?''

"Yes, my lord. With honesty and discretion. The credit to be placed, perhaps, on some other world. It can easily be arranged.'' Scuto fell silent, waiting.

Emil pursed his lips. "You may go,'' he said coldly.

"My lord?''

"You may leave. I gave you my word that you would not be harmed,'' he added. "A Caldor keeps his word. Go now while you are still able.''

From the tower room Emil watched as the trader made his way toward the flitter. It rose with a blur of rotors, faltering a little as it met the strong thermals rising from the surrounding buildings, finally leveling out as it hummed toward the city. He watched as it dwindled in the distance.

Who sent you? he wondered. *The Fentons? The Tomblains? One of the others? Testing me, perhaps. Trying to find some basis for an accusation that I am thinking of breaking the Pact.* His hands clenched as he thought about it. Hive was full of intrigue, with each House striving to get the better of the others and each hampered by the common agreement which held them impotent.

Or had the man been honest? A genuine trader who had made a shrewd guess as to the temptations of the economic system operating on Hive? It would not be hard to do for anyone with imagination and a knowledge of human nature. Such a man could have evaluated the situation, seen the opportunity to make an easy profit and taken a calculated risk by coming out into the open. And it hadn't really been such a terrible risk. He had been guilty of nothing more than offering his services.

But—had the man been genuine?

Derai would have known. Her ability would have searched the root of the trader's motivations. *She should be here*, thought Emil. *I need her now more than ever. The sooner she returns the better and*, he told himself, *once safe in the stronghold she would never be permitted to leave again.*

Her marriage to Ustar would take care of that.

Blaine met the cyber as he climbed the stairs toward the room in which his grandfather spent practically all his time. They faced each other, the tall, hawk-face, and the young person in his dull green tunic picked out with silver. One bore the device of the Caldors, the other the symbol of the Cyclan. One was in the stronghold of his House, the other was basically nothing more than a paid advisor. But neither had any doubt as to who was superior.

"My lord." Automatically the cyber stepped back, yielding the right of way, paying lipservice to protocol and convention.

"A moment." Blaine held out the papers he had carried from the library. "Sergal asked me to give you these."

"Thank you, my lord," said Regor in his soft modulation, the trained voice which contained no irritant factors. "You should not have inconvenienced yourself. The matter is of no urgency."

"A problem?" Blaine was curious. "Something you are doing for Emil?"

"No, my lord. Your uncle was good enough to give his permission for me to examine the data. It is important to keep the mind occupied."

"Yes," said Blaine. "I suppose it is." He was disappointed; here was no ulterior motive, just the desire of the cyber to obtain mental exercise. He looked past the man toward the door of his grandfather's room. "How is he today?"

"The Lord Caldor is very ill, my lord. His illness is one that can yield to no surgery. It is age."

"I know that." Blaine fell silent, thinking. "Tell me," he demanded. "You must know. What is the probability of one or more of the ruling Houses of Hive losing its position? Within a year," he added.

"The probability is very low, my lord."

"Then why is my uncle so worried?"

"That my lord, is a question only he can answer."

It was a rebuke, all the more hurtful because deserved. "Thank you," said Blaine stiffly. "You may go."

Regor bowed, a slight inclination of his head, then went on his way. A member of his retinue guarded his private chambers, a young man, sternly molded, dedicated to the Cyclan and accepting Regor as his master in all things. There was another at food or rest. A third lingered in the city. Three acolytes, a small retinue but sufficient for the purpose. The Cyclan did not make a habit of wasting manpower.

"Maximum seal," ordered Regor. Even command did not harden the soft tones of his voice, but there was no need for aural emphasis. "No interruption of any kind for any reason."

Inside he tossed the papers on a table and entered his private room. Lying supine on the narrow couch he activated the bracelet locked around his left wrist. Invisible power flowed from the instrument and created a field which no spying eye or ear could penetrate. It was a precaution, nothing more, but no cyber ever took the slightest chance when in gestalt communication.

Relaxing, he closed his eyes and concentrated on the Samatchazi formulas. Gradually he lost the sense of taste, smell, touch and hearing. Had he opened his eyes he would have been blind. Locked in his skull, his brain ceased to be irritated by external stimuli. It became a thing of pure intellect, its reasoning awareness its only contact with life. Only then did the engrafted Homochon elements become active. Rapport quickly followed.

Regor became truly alive.

It was the closest any cyber could get to sensual pleasure and even then it was wholly concerned with the mind. Doors opened in the universe and released a tremendous flood of brilliance which was the shining light of eternal truth. He became a living part of an organism which stretched across the galaxy in an infinity of crystalline sparkles, each the glowing nexus of naked intelligence. A skein of misty light connected the whole so that it seemed to be a shifting kaleidoscope of brilliance and form. He saw it and at the same time was a part of it, sharing and yet owning the incredible gestalt of minds.

And somewhere toward the center of that skein was the headquarters of the Cyclan. Buried deep beneath miles of rock, locked and armored in the heart of a lonely planet, the central intelligence absorbed his knowledge as space drank energy. There was no verbal communication; only mental communication in the form of words, quick, practically instantaneous, organic transmission against which the light-beating speed of supra-radio was the merest crawl.

"*Report received and acknowledged. The Caldor girl is on her way to you by commercial vessel. They know of this?*"

An infinitesimal pause.

"*The factor Shamaski notified the House. The man Dumarest is of some interest. There is data on him in my files. Continue with original plan.*"

A comment.

"*Those responsible for permitting the escape of the Caldor girl have been punished.*"

That was all.

The rest was sheer intoxication.

There was always this period after rapport during which the Homochon elements sank back into quiescence and the machinery of the body began to realign itself with mental control. Regor floated in a weightless emptiness while he sensed new and unfamiliar environments, shared strange memories and stranger situations: scraps of overflow from other intelligences, the discard of other minds. The power of central intelligence, the tremendous cybernetic complex which was the mind and heart of the Cyclan.

And of which, one day, he would be part.

IV

THE CASE had dragged too long. Sitting in the high chair of justice Ustar Caldor felt his eyelids grow heavy from both the heat and boredom. Fatigue too, he admitted; there had been no sleep the previous night and little enough the night before that. It was not often that he came into town and he had no intention of wasting his opportunity. Now he should be asleep in readiness for the coming night's pleasure.

He stirred, almost regretting the impulse which had made him insist on his right to oust the resident judge from his chair. And yet, unless such rights were exercised, they quickly became forgotten. Forgetfulness of such a nature was not to be encouraged.

"My lord." The prisoner's advocate was sweating beneath his robe. His client was guilty, of course, but normally he would expect only a small fine or a short term of forced labor. Now? Who could tell what this cold-eyed young man would decide? "My lord," he said again, "I submit that the prosecution has failed to offer evidence to prove that my client is guilty as charged. I realize that the onus of proof is ours to show that we are guiltless and this we have failed to do. In such circumstances, my lord, we have no alternative than to throw ourselves on your mercy."

Ustar sat, brooding. *They could have done this in the first place,* he thought, *and saved us all a lot of time and discomfort.* He looked at the prisoner, a small trader who had cheated on his returns and thus robbed the

House of needed revenue. Well, how to punish the man? How to show both the strength and justice of the Caldors?

"The fine will be sixty times the amount stolen," he announced. "The sentence will be three years at forced labor."

The prisoner blanched.

"My lord!" The advocate had courage. "The sentence is extreme, my lord," he said. "I beg you to reconsider your decision!"

"You condone his theft?" Ustar was deceptively mild. "You, a member of the House of Caldor, consider that this man is undeserving of punishment?"

"No, my lord, but—"

"He stole from the House," said Ustar, interrupting. "He stole from me, from you, from us all. The amount is insignificant. The sentence stands."

"My lord." The advocate bowed, accepting defeat. It was going to be an unlucky day for those coming to trial.

The morning dragged. Shortly after midday Ustar adjourned the court in order to take a bath and eat some much-needed food. He was on his main course when a shadow fell across his plate. Looking up he saw the resident judge. "May I speak with you, my lord?"

"Sit down." Ustar gestured toward an empty chair. "Let's get one thing clear. I do not intend to argue about the decisions I have made. Understand?"

"I did not wish to speak to you about that." The judge was old and had learned patience. "Your grandfather," he said. "We rarely see him in town. Is he well?"

"As well as can be expected."

"And your father?"

"The same." Ustar pushed away his empty plate. He

was amused at the other's discomfiture but did nothing to ease it. It was as well that such men as the judge should be reminded as to who were their masters. "I have been thinking," he said abruptly. "The scale of fines as laid down by the court seems far too low. As a source of revenue they have been sadly neglected."

"Fines are not intended to be revenue, my lord. They are a means of punishing minor offenders."

"Even so they are still too low. I suggest that you treble them immediately." Ustar poured himself wine. "The sentences too. They should also be increased."

"Sentences vary, my lord," said the judge patiently. "As crimes vary. Justice must always be tempered with understanding and mercy. Age will teach you that," he added. "And experience."

Ustar sipped his wine. The old man had courage, he admitted to himself, perhaps too much courage. "I am young," he said. "True, but I am not necessarily a fool because of that. Caldor needs money and your court is a means of getting it. We could arrange to remit sentences," he suggested. "Hit wealthy men hard and then let them buy themselves off. So much for a day, a week, a year. It has possibilities."

He was, thought the judge, like a child with a new toy. A vicious child with a very delicate toy. Vicious or just careless, the results would be the same. For Caldor justice would become a bad word. Deliberately he changed the subject. "Do you intend to stay long in town, my lord?"

Ustar drank more wine, tempted to continue the suspense, then abruptly tiring of the game. "I am waiting for the Lady Derai," he explained. "Her ship should be arriving at any time. In fact," he added as a familiar sound echoed from the sky, "this could be it now."

But there was still ample time to finish the meal.

The agent was a Hausi, plump, bland, smiling like a cat, caste marks livid against the ebon of his skin. He stood in the blazing sunlight halfway between the ship and the edge of the field, his voice cheerful as he shouted his offer. "Five! Five a day! I can use every able-bodied man!"

Dumarest paused, watching. Beside him the girl moved with restless impatience.

"Come on, Earl. He's just recruiting labor for the harvest. It's of no interest to you."

Dumarest didn't answer. His eyes were busy searching the sky, the field, the city beyond. The sky was a hard, clear blue, the sun a brazen disc of searing brilliance, the air hot and sticky with tropic warmth. The field was gravel, tamped hard and kept clean and level. A group of men worked at it, heads bowed, shuffling in a familiar way. Other men stood and watched them. Prisoners and their guards. Well, it was usual to use convict labor to maintain the fields.

"Come on, Earl," urged Derai impatiently. "Let's get home."

"A moment." The city was interesting. It reached to the edge of the field, a sprawling collection of shops, houses, small factories and stores. It seemed to have no trace of planning or design. A few roads ran from it, none very far. To the field, the warehouses humped around the central square, the long, low sheds to one side. It looked more like an overgrown village than a thriving metropolis.

He would do his business and be on his way. Instinct warned him that Hive was not a good world on which to linger.

"Your first time on Hive, sir?" The agent was

courteous. "An interesting world. There are those, perhaps, with greater impact on the senses but few with so much subtle beauty to entrance the beholder. I could arrange a tour of inspection for yourself and your lady. Modern air-transports and an accomplished guide. My card, sir. The name is Yamay Mbombo. I am well known in the town, sir. A question at any hotel or tavern will yield my address. Shall I book you now for our special three-day survey?"

Dumarest shook his head. "Thank you, no."

"As you wish, sir." The Hausi turned to look at a knot of men slowly approaching from the ship. "Five!" he called. "Five a day! I can use every able-bodied man!"

"Five." Dumarest was thoughtful. It seemed low. "Tell me," he said to the girl, "how much will that buy on Hive?"

"How should I know?"

"Find out," he suggested. "Read his mind." And then, after a moment, "Well?"

"A lot," she said, and shuddered. "It was horrible," she complained. "Beastly!"

"He is probably married to one or more women," said Dumarest calmly. "He could even be hungry. When are you going to learn that subconscious thoughts have nothing to do with intended action? We are all of us beasts," he added. "Most of us learn to correctly judge what we see and hear." It was a lesson he had tried to teach her during the entire journey. He'd had little success.

"Why are we waiting?" Derai caught him by the arm and pressed her body close to his own. There was nothing childish in the gesture. "You kept us waiting on the ship," she complained. "We were the last to leave. We could have been home by now."

"Be patient," said Dumarest. He felt uneasy. Hive, apparently, was a poor world. He turned to examine the group of those who had traveled Low. They were thin, pale, barely recovered from resurrection. Some would have a little money, enough perhaps to tide them over until they could find employment. Some lacked even that. All were strangers. "All right," he said to the girl. "We can go now."

Dumarest narrowed his eyes as they approached the gate. A cluster of people stood before it on the anyman's-land of the field. A row of sagging tents and flimsy structures reached along the fence to either side, again on the field-side of the high wire mesh. A portable church of the Universal Brotherhood stood at a small distance from the furthest tent and Dumarest could spot the drab homespun of a monk among the people.

A man turned as they approached. He was flushed, nervous, eyes bright with panic. Sar Eldon was in a bad way. "Dumarest!" He swallowed and tried to control his voice. "Thank God for a friendly face. I thought you'd gone, that I was all alone." He broke off and wiped the perspiration from his face. "I hate asking this," he said flatly. "But I've got no choice. Will you please lend me some money?"

Dumarest was curt. "You had money. More than the cost of your passage."

"The captain took it all. He said that I owed it to him. Now I know why." Eldon jerked his head toward the gate. "They won't let me out," he explained. "I haven't got the landing fee. I've got the choice of staying here," he continued. "Living like the rest of them inside the field. Or I can crawl back to the ship and beg them to take me back. If I do that I'll have to take whatever terms the captain offers. I'll be a slave for life.''

''And the rest?''

''Worse. They have no chance to ship out.'' The gambler, for once, was honest.

Dumarest looked at the others. They were a familiar sight. Dressed in rags, emaciated, literally starving. Men without money and so without hope; travelers who had hit the end of the line, barred from leaving the field in order to seek employment or search for food. *Hive*, he thought grimly, *promised to be a place to remember*.

''Earl.'' He felt the tug at his arm and became conscious of the girl at his side. Her face was twisted as if with pain but she was free of fear. He was glad of that. ''Earl, why are all these people so miserable?''

''They are starving,'' he explained. ''Your people are watching them starve.'' It was unfair but true. Too many of the aristocracy went on their way blind to the suffering of others. For her there was no excuse.

''We must help them,'' she decided. ''Earl, what is it they need?''

''Money.''

''You have money.'' To her the situation was childishly simple. ''If you give it to them they will no longer suffer. Is that correct?''

''It is. For a time,'' he added. ''I cannot promise as to the future. But, in this case, charity seems unnecessary.'' He moved closer to the crowd and caught a man by the shoulder. ''You want money,'' he said. ''There is an agent on the field offering employment. Why don't you accept it?''

''At five a day?''

''At one a day if you have to. If that's all there is to take. Or do you prefer to sit here and starve?''

"No," said the man. He was small, with a straggling mane of red hair and a face smothered with freckles beneath the dirt. "No," he repeated. "I don't prefer that at all. But I'm damned if I'm going to risk my neck just to pay their landing fees. Landing fees!" He spat on the gravel. "Where else would you find such a racket? I've been on a hundred worlds and I've never met up with this before." He spat again and glared at Dumarest. "We were talking about work," he said. "Do you know what kind of work he's offering?"

"Something to do with harvesting."

"That's right, but do you know what? The jelly," said the man. "The stuff they sell for a fortune. They pay five a day and if one out of two men live to collect it they reckon they've made a bad deal. Five a day for a fifty percent chance of getting killed. Would you take it?"

"I don't know," said Dumarest. "But I can't blame you for thinking about it."

He stepped back and looked beyond the gate. Outside a crowd of casual watchers stood behind the cluster of guards. Most of them, he noticed, wore a tunic of varying color, each bearing a blazon on the left breast. A few wore heavy daggers at their belts, symbols of authority or a badge of rank. Derai pulled at his arm.

"Earl," she insisted, "do something for these people. I will repay," she said quickly. "My House is not poor. I ask you only to lend me the money until we reach home. Please, Earl!" Her hand tightened on his arm. "For me," she whispered. "Do it for me."

The church was small, the benediction light the most prominent object, the hypnotic device before which the supplicants sat, confessing their sins and receiving subjective penance before being given the bread of forgiveness. Beyond it, in the confessional, sat Brother

Yitrium. He looked little different from the rest. His robe was patched and his person clean, but his face showed the signs of deprivation. Now he sat, head bowed, praying.

"Brother," he said finally to Dumarest, "what can I say? Each time I leave the field I have to pay the charge. We have no established church on this planet and the Houses are not sympathetic to our teaching. I had begun to believe, God help me, that charity was dead. Now I see that it is not."

"How much?" said Dumarest. "Not just to clear the field, I can count that for myself, but to give them enough so that they stand a chance of getting on their feet outside."

"Give him all that you have," said Derai impatiently. "You won't need it now."

"We have yet to leave the field," reminded Dumarest.

"I am of the House of Caldor!" Here her pride had some meaning. "They would not dare to demand a charge from me or those with me. Give him the money. All of it. Quickly, so that we can get home."

Home, thought Dumarest bleakly, *and the inevitable parting*. He would miss her. He poured coins into the monk's bowl.

"Bless you, brother," said the monk.

"Bless her," said Dumarest dryly. "It's her money."

Outside, back at the gate, things had altered. Most of the watchers had gone. Those inside had resumed their positions at the fence calling out to those who passed, begging for food and money. The agent had gone. The area around the ship was deserted. Eldon was the only familiar face in sight.

"Dumarest! For God's sake—"

"You'll get out. The monk has money for you all."
Dumarest turned to Derai. "Shall we go?"

"Yes," she said. And took three steps. And paused.
"Ustar!"

"In the flesh, sweet cousin." He stepped arrogantly
through the gate. "I had almost given you up but then I
checked and found you had traveled on this vessel." He
looked once at Dumarest. "I trust that you had a pleasant journey?"

"Most enjoyable."

"I am glad to hear it. Sometimes these journeys can
be such a bore. You probably found a means of amusing
yourself. But now the journey is over."

He came closer, very tall, very confident, impecca-
ble in his tunic of dull green blazoned with silver. His
hand rested lightly on the hilt of his dagger *but,* thought
Dumarest, *to him it is more than a symbol. He knows
how to use it and is probably spoiling to use it again.*

"My lady—" he began, but she gestured him to
silence.

"Ustar," she said. "It is most kind of you to have
met me. My father, he is well?"

"Both he and your half-brother." Ustar extended his
arm, ignoring Dumarest as if he were part of the scen-
ery. "I have a flitter waiting. We can be home in a very
short while. Come, Derai."

She took his arm and fell into step beside him.
Dumarest followed to be abruptly halted by a guard.
"Your fee," said the man. "You haven't paid it."

"It will be paid," said Dumarest. Money, now, was
important. Bleakly he stared after the couple; not once
did she turn her head.

So much for the gratitude of princes.

The room had a bitter, medical smell, the odor of

drugs, age and senile decay. *It was imagination,* thought Johan. The place was spotless, well-aired, scented with the perfume of wild rose and osphage. It could not smell of illness and incipient death. But, somehow, it did. The Old Man had even managed to impress his personality on this, the limited area of his final sovereignty, the room in which he would die.

Johan turned as a nurse moved softly toward the figure on the pneumatic mattress, made a routine check, moved quietly back to her seat beside the door. She knew, of course, as did the physician, the cyber, Emil and himself. Perhaps there were others but, if so, they knew better than to speak of what they knew. Each House contained at least one resident similar to the Old Man.

Johan moved toward the bed. The figure lying supine was gross, bloated, a swollen bag of tissue in which still pounded a living heart, still operated a pair of lungs. *And which,* he thought sickly, *still housed a living brain. My father,* he told himself cynically; it was near enough to the truth. But his father was dead. His grandfather was dead. The figure in the bed was his great-grandfather. The lucky one. The legend. The perpetual grandfather. The man who had managed to stretch his life across generations, extending it by the undiluted magic of ambrosaira, the royal jelly of the mutated bees.

Extended it—for what?

A faint sound came from the bed. A thin wheezing, a rasping, a horrible liquid gurgling. At once the nurse was at her station, fingers deft as she administered drugs, soothing the erratic jerkings of the monstrous body. *He wants something,* thought Johan. *He is trying to communicate. But his vocal chords are gone, his coordination, the synchronization between brain and body. He is worse than a cabbage,* he told himself. *At least a vegetable does not realize that it waits simply to die.*

He looked up as the door softly opened. Blaine stood at the threshold. His natural son, the first fruit of diverse love and the wonderful initial proof that his genes were still viable, still able to fertilize an ovum. He'd celebrated the night Blaine had been born by managing to get unaccustomedly drunk. When he'd recovered the boy's mother had vanished, never again to be seen.

He had not touched wine since.

"Father." The boy kept his voice low and Johan was glad of that. It showed respect if nothing else. "Derai is home," he said. "Ustar brought her from the field."

"Derai? Home?" Johan crossed the room, almost running in his eagerness. "Why wasn't I told that she was expected?" He could guess the reason. It was more of Emil's work and his face darkened as he thought about it. The man was taking too much on himself. Perhaps it was time he asserted his authority. But that could come later. First he had to see his daughter.

"Father!" She held him in her arms. "It is good to be back. You can't guess how much I've missed you."

"And I've missed you too, daughter." He stepped back and looked at her. She had changed but he could not decide just how or in what manner. There was a certain self-assurance which had previously been lacking, a calmness which he did not remember. Perhaps Regor had been correct in his suggestion that the Cyclan college at Huen would be of assistance. But why had she run away from it?

"Later," she said, before he could ask the question. "I'll tell you later. When we are alone."

It was hours before that happened. Ustar, like an irritating burr, insisted on keeping them company, dulling their ears with his tales of fancied prowess. Emil was just as bad; he seemed to have something on his mind. Regor, after paying his respects, had retired to his chambers. He, at least, had shown politeness, thought Johan. He hadn't even asked her why she had left the college. Finally they were alone.

"I was terrified," she said. "I had to run away. I was afraid for my life."

"Imagination, child?"

"I don't know. I don't think so. They are such strange people," she said. "The cybers, I mean. So cold. So devoid of emotion. They are just like machines."

"They are machines," he said. "Thinking mechanisms of flesh and blood. They are trained to extrapolate from known data and to predict the logical outcome of any action or sequence of events. That is why they are such good advisors. They are always neutral and can always be trusted. But they do not consider emotion to be workable data. Therefore they ignore it." *And therefore,* he added silently to himself, *they ignore the major part of human existence.* "It was a mistake sending you to the college," he admitted. "But Emil was so insistent that it would do you good. Regor too. And," he finished, "they appear to have been right. You have changed."

"I feel different," she admitted. "But that has nothing to do with the college. Promise me that you will not send me back."

"I promise."

"I owe the factor on Kyle some money," she said. "I told him the House would repay his expenses."

"It will be attended to."

They talked more, about inconsequentialities mostly, noise to fill the silence. And then, when it was very late, he insisted that it was time for bed.

"Must I, Father? So soon?"

"It's late," he insisted. "And you must be tired."

"I don't feel tired." She stretched, throwing back
her head so that the cascade of her hair hung unre-
stricted down her back. "Father, there is something I
must tell you."

"Is it important?" He stifled a yawn. "Could it wait
until tomorrow?"

"Yes," she said. "Of course it can wait. Good
night, Father."

"Good night."

Perhaps she really is better, he thought as he left her
room. *Perhaps the college did help, even though she
doesn't admit it. It could be that her desire to run was
the culmination of the treatment.*

But from what she had told him it had been a peculiar
kind of treatment. Tests both physical and mental with
particular reference to her fertility and chromosome
pattern, as if they were more interested in her as a
breeding animal than a patient they were trying to help.

Still, he consoled himself, *she does appear to be
more stable.* Even if she had only learned to rationalize
her previously ungovernable fear it would help. He
remembered too vividly the nights when she had waked
him with her frantic screams. The long nights when
she'd had to be drugged into silence.

It had been that more than anything else which had
persuaded him to agree to Emil's suggestion.

Tiredly he crept into his bed. It had been a long day.
Tomorrow he would consider what was best for him to
do. Tomorrow—after a good night's sleep.

But that night Derai woke and tore the air with her
screams.

V

YAMAY MBOMBO had an office on the second floor of a crumbling building made of timber and stone. It was an unpretentious place, poorly furnished, but Dumarest knew better than to take it at face value. Few of the Hausi were poor. The agent smiled from behind a desk as he entered. "It is good to see you again, Dumarest, sir."

"You know me?"

Yamay's smile grew wider. "We have a mutual friend, a gambler. He came to me with an interesting proposition. From him I learned how it was that I found it impossible to recruit labor to fill my contract."

"You should offer more," said Dumarest without sympathy. He found a chair and sat down. "Do you hold me to blame?"

"Of course not, my dear sir. In fact, it is to my advantage. Now I will have reason to persuade my employers to offer higher fees and that will mean a larger commission. You have done me a favor. In return I offer you some advice: the walls of portable churches are very thin." The agent looked critically at his fingernails. "I take it," he said softly, "that you did not dispose of all your wealth as the girl requested?"

"No."

"I thought not. You are a man of sense. You realize how easy it is for others to be generous when it is not their money at stake. The girl belongs to a House, does

she not?'' The agent shrugged at Dumarest's nod.
"Well," he admitted, "it is barely possible that you
may yet be repaid. In which case you will naturally add
something to the sum you actually gave to the monk and
so make a legitimate profit."

Dumarest was ironic. "Legitimate?"

"Just so." The Hausi was serious. "Money loaned
at such risk deserves to carry a high rate of interest.
Need I explain that the Houses frown on usury?"
Yamay straightened and looked at Dumarest. "A man
must make his profit as best he can. On this planet he
makes it or he does not live. But we digress. Why have
you come to me?"

"For help," said Dumarest, and added, "I can pay
for it."

"Then you shall have it," said the Hausi. "Anything
you require that is within my power to give. You want
information? I am the one who can give it. You would
like a drink? I can give you that too." Opening a
drawer, the agent produced a bottle and two glasses. He
poured and pushed one across the desk to Dumarest.
"Your health, sir!"

The liquid was strong, with an underlying acrid
flavor and heavy with sweetness.

"Honey," said the agent. "On Hive you rapidly
grow accustomed to the taste. Hive," he repeated. "A
peculiar world."

"So I've gathered." Dumarest had spent some time
looking around. He was unimpressed by what he had
seen. "Why is it so poor?"

"The usual reason—far too many hands dipping into
the pot." The agent poured more drinks. "This world
was first settled by twenty-nine families," he
explained. "Six died out within the first decade. The
rest survived to fight like starving dogs over a single

bone. War," he reminded, "is never profitable for those who engage in actual combat. Finally even the hotheaded fools who run the Houses recognized that they were on the road to mutual destruction. So those Houses that remained, eleven of them, signed the Pact. If one House is attacked the rest will combine against the attacker, destroy it and, presumably, share the loot. As yet it hasn't happened but it is an uneasy peace."

"A feudal system," said Dumarest. "Class, privilege and selfish greed. I've seen it before."

"On many worlds, no doubt," agreed the agent. "But you see now why Hive is so poor. What else when every lord entitled to wear the dagger is a stranger to work and yet must have his servants, his luxuries, his imported goods and expensive tours to other planets? The produced wealth cannot meet the demand. So those who have little are forced to accept even less. I predict," said Yamay, "that the critical point of disruption is very close. Certainly within the next generation."

"Inter-House war," said Dumarest. "Revolution. Chaos."

"And then, perhaps, expansion, growth and a proper exploitation of this planet." The agent drank, waited for Dumarest to follow his example, then refilled the glasses. "But to business. What can I do for you?"

"I want transportation," said Dumarest. "To a village or town called Lausary. You know it?"

The Hausi frowned. "Lausary," he murmured. "Lausary. It strikes a familiar note but I cannot immediately place it." He rose and glowered at a map pinned to the wall. "Was it the place you wanted or someone within it?"

"A man. I understand he is to be found there."

"This man. What is his House? The color of his tunic? His blazon?"

"I don't know. I've never met him." Dumarest rose. "Well, if you can't help me—"

"I did not say that!" Yamay was touched on his professional pride. He jabbed a thumb at the intercom on his desk. "Faine! Come in here. Fast!"

Faine was a squat, middle-aged man with thinning hair and blunt fingers stained with grease. He nodded at Dumarest, then looked at the agent.

"Lausary," said Yamay. "This gentleman wants to go there. You know it?"

"Sure," said Faine. "It's a small settlement deep in the Freelands. About ten miles west of Major Peak. That's why you don't know it. You don't run tours out there." He looked at Dumarest. "When did you want to go?"

"Right away."

Faine looked dubious. "It's getting late," he said. "We'll have to camp out for the night, but if you don't mind that I'm willing."

"How much?" asked Dumarest. He stared when the agent told him. "Look," he said reasonably, "I don't want to buy the flitter. I just want transportation there and back."

"That is understood," said Yamay quickly. "And I assure you that the charter fee is not exorbitant. The balance is for a deposit. The flitter is this man's livelihood," he explained. "The Freelands are not the safest place in which to venture. The deposit is an insurance against damage."

"And if I should refuse to pay it?"

Yamay's shrug was expressive. If Dumarest wanted to go he would pay.

"Thank you, Dumarest, sir." The agent beamed as he counted the money. "It is a pleasure to do business

with such a man. Is there anything else I can do for
you?''

"Yes," said Dumarest. "You can give me a re-
ceipt.''

The flitter was old, worn, the rotors unevenly balanced so that the craft jerked and vibrated as it limped
slowly through the air. Dumarest wondered at the use of
such primitive transport but he could guess the reason.
Anti-grav rafts were simple, effective and economical
on power but they would give their owners a freedom
unpalatable to those who ruled the planet.

He looked through the transparent cabin at the
ground below. It had changed from fertile soil and
well-tended fields to a stony, rugged expanse dotted
with huge boulders and scarred with shallow gullies.
The sun had almost set, lying blood red on the horizon,
throwing long shadows over the terrain. Spined plants
grew in scattered clumps, straggling ugly things with
knotted stems bearing sickly white blooms as large as a
man's head.

"Osphage," said Faine. It was the first time he had
spoken since they had left the city. "It grows a lot
thicker down south in the Freelands. It's about the only
thing that does grow. That and the bees. The bad kind.''

Dumarest sensed the other's desire for conversation.
"You have more than one kind?''

"Sure. There's the small one, the kind that can be
bred and handled and put to useful work. And there's
the other kind, which breeds in the Freelands. If you see
them coming you dive for cover and don't waste time
doing it. If you don't they'll kill you. They swarm," he
explained. "They like to find something hollow to
serve as a nest. Sometimes it's a house. When that

happens the owners have a choice. They can kill the swarm or they can move. Usually they move.''

"Why don't they keep moving?'' Dumarest was only vaguely interested. "Move right out of the Freelands if they're so bad.''

"They're bad enough.'' Faine slammed shut the airvent on his side of the cabin. "So bad that even the Houses didn't want them. They left them as a sort of no-man's-land. Lawbreakers and people on the run learned they were safe there. Safe from the Houses, that is. Others joined them, retainers of vanquished Houses, deserters, stranded travelers, people like that.'' He looked at Dumarest. "They stayed and settled and managed to survive. Don't ask me how.''

"They probably wanted to live,'' said Dumarest dryly. "What's so bad about the place?''

"It's hot. Radioactive. Maybe because of some old war or it could be natural. That's why the osphage grows so thick down there. That's what mutated the bees. That's why the population stays so low. I've seen some of their newborn. It was a mercy to let them die.''

Dumarest twisted in his seat. The cover was worn, the padding uneven and the thing sagged, but it was comfortable enough. Against the sky a flock of what he took to be birds drew a thin line of darkness across the sun. The shadows grew longer, distorting the detail below so that they seemed to be flying into a strange universe of unfamiliar shapes. Faine grunted and adjusted his controls. The beat of the engine altered as the flitter slowed and began to ease toward the ground.

"We'll land,'' he said. "Settle for the night.''

"So soon?''

"It gets dark pretty quick once the sun has gone down. I don't want to risk smashing the crate on one of those boulders.''

They landed in a clear space well away from big stones, gullies and spined trees. Faine rummaged in a box and produced a wrapped packet of sandwiches and a couple of bottles of wine. He handed one to Dumarest and divided the sandwiches. "It isn't much," he apologized. "The wife was a little short of funds."

The bread was stale, the filling tasteless. The wine was barely drinkable. It was, Dumarest decided, more of a honey beer than true wine and was obviously homemade. But it was food and drink.

"Who are you looking for in Lausary?" asked Faine after they had eaten. "A friend?"

"Just someone I want to meet."

"A traveler like yourself?"

Dumarest ignored the question, easing himself in the chair in which he would spend the night. Faine had vetoed his suggestion that they sleep outside. They would stay in the cabin, he insisted. Where it was safe. He did not say safe from what and Dumarest hadn't asked. He assumed the man knew his own planet.

"I just thought that I might know him," said Faine. He paused. "I was a traveler once myself," he said abruptly. "I drifted around for a while until I landed here. That was sixteen years ago. I met a girl and my traveling days were over." He sat, brooding in the starlit darkness. "I thought I had it made," he continued. "I'm a mechanic and a good one. I opened a shop and thought I'd get rich but it didn't work out that way. Ordinary people can't afford to own their own machines and the Houses have their own service engineers. Things were pretty bad when I met up with Yamay. I maintain his fleet and he gives me some extra work on the side. Like this trip," he explained. "He wouldn't touch it himself."

"Why not?" Dumarest looked at the other man. His

face was a pale blur in the darkness of the cabin. On the instrument panel faded luminosity traced ghost-patterns of battered dials. "And why did we have to camp? Couldn't we have made it in one hop?"

"We could," admitted Faine. "But what if something had happened? A rotor come adrift, maybe, or something else? Starlight's deceptive and the ground is pretty rugged. We'd have cracked up for certain. That's why Yamay gave me the job. He didn't want to risk one of his own flitters. But you don't have to worry," he said. "We can make an early start, hit Lausary in good time for you to do your business and be back in town before nightfall."

Dumarest turned over on his side.

"That deposit," said Faine. "I don't want you to get the wrong idea about that."

"I won't." Dumarest was grim; it had taken practically all his money. "Not while you're doing the piloting. If you smash the ship it's your fault, not mine."

"Sure," said Faine. "I'm not arguing about that. But it's there in case something happens that isn't my fault. The Freelands can be pretty rough." He craned forward, head twisted to stare at Dumarest. "Look," he said urgently. "I'm thinking of the wife. I—"

"Go to sleep," said Dumarest.

Faine sighed, the chair creaking as he shifted his weight.

"Good night."

For a long time Dumarest lay awake looking up through the transparent roof of the cabin. The sky was clear, the stars glittered from horizon to horizon, thick as the stones of the desert, great suns and nebulas, streamers and curtains of luminous gas as bright, as silver, as a woman's hair. A very special kind of woman.

He fell asleep thinking of Derai.

The fear was a cloud, a sea, an ebony mist which wound itself closer, tighter, trapping, smothering, encysting in a world of naked terror. There was no light, no sound, nothing but the darkness and the fear. The dreadful fear, so encompassing that her mind edged at the limits of sanity in an effort to escape.

And always, always, was the soundless, wordless, incoherent screaming.

"Derai!"

She felt her throat grow raw from echoing the screams.

"Derai!"

She felt the arms, heard the voice, opened her eyes and saw the light, the blessed light. "Father!"

"There, there, my child." His words were soothing but louder than the words came his thoughts underlaid by his emotions. *What's wrong with her? Why does she scream? I thought all this was over.* Tenderness, anxiety, a desire to protect and an empty helplessness. "It's all right, Derai," he said. "It's all right."

"Derai!" Blaine came running into the bedchamber. Like Johan he wore a robe over his nightclothes. "Is anything wrong?" *She's having nightmares again. The poor kid. Why can't they do something to help her?* The desire to protect. The desire to help. The sympathy of understanding.

Another thought, ice-cold, striking like a knife:

The stupid bitch! What's wrong with her now? What a way for a Caldor to behave! Impatience, irritation and contempt. "My sweet cousin!" Ustar entered the room. He was fully dressed, his dagger naked in his hand. "I heard the screams," he said to Johan. "I thought there might be danger." He stepped to the side

of the bed, knelt, let the dagger fall to the carpet.
"Derai, my dearest!" His hands reached for her own.
"You were having a nightmare," he said confidently.
"The strain of travel must have upset you. It's natural
enough." His hands were tight, possessive as they
gripped her own. "But you are safe here in the stronghold. No one can hurt you now."

"Is everything all right?" Emil, blinking, but, like
his son, fully dressed, entered the room, the physician
at his heels. Trudo set down the bag he carried, opened
it, reached inside for his hypogun. To him this was a
familiar scene but still he felt pity.

Derai felt more. A flood of thoughts and conflicting
emotions made a blur of mental sound and intangible
violence. A crowd shouting at the top of its voice in the
confines of a small room. And still she could hear the
dreadful, soundless, mindless screaming.

Hear it and echo it.

"Derai!" Johan was pale with anxiety. "Stop it!
Please stop it!"

"Give her something." Ustar released her hands and
turned to the physician. "Something to keep her quiet.
Hurry man!"

"Yes, my lord." Trudo stepped forward, the hypogun in his hand. He paused as someone spoke from the
door.

"Could I be of assistance?" Regor stood just within
the chamber and the cyber immediately dominated the
room. He was tall, self-possessed, a commanding figure in his scarlet robe, the Cyclan seal blazoned on its
breast. He was polite, his tones the same even modulation, but he could not be ignored. He stepped forward,
gesturing the physician to one side, taking Ustar's place
at the side of the bed. Reaching forward, he placed his
hands to either side of the girl's head. From the shadow

of his cowl he stared into her face. "Look at me!" he said. "Look at me!"

Her eyes were wild, unfocused, her muscles rigid with hysteria.

"Look at me," he said again, and his fingers moved deftly at the base of her skull. "Look at me! Look at me! I will help but you must look at me!" Assurance. Certainty. The absolute conviction that what he did was right. The power of his directed thought overwhelmed the noise and confusion, driving the mindless scream-ing back into the general blur of mental sound.

Derai stopped screaming. She relaxed a little, meet-ing his eyes, recognizing his desire to help.

"You will relax," he said gently. "You will cease to be afraid. You will trust me to see that you come to no harm. You will relax," he said again. "You will re-lax."

She sighed and obeyed. Of them all the cyber was the most comforting. More so even than her father for his thoughts were stained with a patina of emotion and the cyber had none. Regor was coldly precise. He consid-ered her, she thought, dreamily, as a piece of prop-erty. A rare and valuable example of biological en-gineering. And then, suddenly, she remembered the Cyclan college and the reason she had run away.

Trudo slowly packed his bag. It was old, worn, the fastenings inclined to jam, but it was familiar and held close associations and he was reluctant to change it for another. He checked the hypogun and slid it into place. It too was old, the nozzle worn, the calibration not as fine as he would have wished. Johan had given it to him as a present to mark the occasion of Derai's birth.

He looked to where she lay on the bed. Quiet now, drugged, sedated into artificial sleep. Her hair shone as it wreathed her face. *She looks so young*, he thought, *so helpless*. But appearances were deceptive. She was older than she looked and was far from defenseless. Vulnerable, perhaps, but that was partly her own fault. Had her mother lived things could have been different. But her mother had not lived and he didn't like to remember that dreadful night when he had watched her die.

And yet Johan had still given him the present. Another lord would have thrown him from the turret with a noose around his neck. Emil, for instance, or his son. But Ustar's mother had died in a flitter crash ten years after he was born.

"We should do something," said Ustar. "This can't be allowed to continue." His voice was hard, positive.

"What do you suggest?" Johan sat beside the bed, one hand touching that of his daughter. He felt and sounded very old. His throat tightened as he remembered the screams, the frantic writhings, the almost incoherent noises before the physician had used his drugs. Was it to continue the same as before? How long could she cling to sanity?

"There must be something," said Ustar. "A brain operation, lobotomy, something like that." He looked at the physician. "Could such a thing be done?"

"Yes, my lord."

"Would it cure her of these nightmares?"

"It would alter her personality," said the doctor cautiously. "It would make her insensitive to fear."

"With respect, my lord." Regor stepped forward. A scarlet flame in the soft illumination of the room. "It would be a mistake to attempt any such operation," he said evenly. "It would destroy, not create. There are other solutions to this problem."

"Such as your college, cyber?" Ustar made no attempt to hide his sneer. "They do not seem to have had much success."

"Nevertheless, it would be most unwise to tamper with her brain."

"Of course it would," said Emil. "You're tired," he said to his son. "I suggest we retire. Good night, Johan."

In the seclusion of his chamber he looked balefully at his only child. "Do you have to act like an utter fool?"

Ustar flushed.

"You suggest operating on her brain—if you do that you destroy the one thing which makes her valuable. And she knows how you feel. Do you think that will endear her to you as a bride?"

"Do I have to marry her?"

"You have no choice—not if you hope to become Head of the House of Caldor." Irritably Emil paced the room. Why had he sired such a fool? What turn of fate had made his seed so infertile that he was practically sterile? "Listen," he said. "Things are moving toward a climax. We either remain one of the ruling Houses or we lose everything we have. It is a time for strong leadership. You must provide it. Aided," he added, "by my advice."

"The power behind the throne?" Ustar looked at his father. *That's what he wants,* he told himself. *That's what he hopes to get: the actual rule. Because he can never get it himself, he has to work through me. And that,* he thought smugly, *makes me pretty important.* "There are other ways," he said. "I don't have to marry that freak. The Old Man could die."

"And then Johan would Head the House." Emil was ahead of his son. "Oh, he could die too—I've thought about it. But what then? I would never be allowed to take over. There are too many jealous relatives to see to that—not while Derai is the natural successor. They would back her . . . a woman," he said. "A soft, weak, pliable woman in control of the House at a time when it needs the full strength of a man. A mature man," he added. "Someone with experience and skill in political maneuvering."

"If Johan should die," said Ustar thoughtfully, "then Derai could die also."

"She could," admitted Emil. "But not until you are married and she has given you a child. You would then be in the position of regent. But why kill her at all? Why not use her instead?" He paced the floor, letting Ustar think about if, then returned to stare at his son. "You are a fine-looking man," he said dispassionately. "It shouldn't be hard for you to turn the head and win the heart of a young girl. Not when the rewards are so high. Not when you have no competition."

Ustar smiled, preening himself.

"But you must control your mind," warned Emil. "You must think and believe what you say." He paused, frowning. "That name," he said. "When Derai was screaming and struggling in Regor's hands she called out something. A name."

"Earl," Ustar remembered.

"A man's name. Do you know him?"

"No," said Ustar. "Not personally. But she traveled with a man, Earl Dumarest. His name was on the passenger list." He paused, frowning. "He accompanied her to the gate. I saw him. Some cheap traveler lying his way into her good graces."

Emil sighed; would the fool never learn that you couldn't lie to a telepath? But the information was disturbing. He said so and Ustar shrugged.

"A cheap traveler," he repeated. "A nothing. A nobody. What importance could he have?"

"She called his name," Emil pointed out. "At a time of acute anxiety and fear she called his name. It is quite possible that she has formed a romantic attachment to this man. In which case," he added significantly, "it would be wise for you to do something about it."

Ustar dropped his hand to his dagger.

"That's right," said Emil. "And soon."

VI

LAUSARY was a cluster of about thirty houses, two sheds, a store and what seemed to be a communal meeting place with a wide veranda and a low tower in which swung a bell. They reached it an hour after dawn and hovered, watching.

"There's something wrong," said Dumarest. He narrowed his eyes against the sun-glare and looked to the east. Long rows of cultivated osphage reached to a low ridge of crumbled stone. To the north and south it was much the same. The west held neat patches of various crops, each patch sitting in its own catchment basin. Nowhere was there a sign of life.

"It's still early," said Faine uncertainly. "Maybe they're not up yet."

"They're farmers." Dumarest leaned from the flitter looking down at a small patch of cleared ground which obviously served as a landing field. "In a place like this they'd be up at first light." He pulled in his head and looked at the pilot. "When did you call here last?"

"A few weeks ago. It was afternoon."

"And before that?"

"About three months. I came this way heading toward Major Peak. You can see it over there." He pointed to the east. "That was early morning," he admitted. "They were up and working then." He looked dubiously at the village below. "What do we do?"

"We land."

"But—"

"We land."

Silence followed the cutting of the engine. A deep, unnatural silence for any village. Even if there were no dogs or other animals there should have been sound of some kind. A laugh, a snore, the movement of people rising to their labors. Here there was nothing.

"I don't like this," said Faine. "I don't like it at all." His boots made crunching sounds as he came to stand beside Dumarest. In one hand he carried a heavy machete. Dumarest looked at the blade.

"What's that for?"

"Comfort," admitted the pilot. He stared at the silent dwellings. "If they'd been taken over by a swarm," he said, "you'd know it. You can hear the damn things yards away. But what else? Plague, perhaps?"

"There's only one way to find out," said Dumarest. "I'll take this side, you take the other. Look in every house, every room. If you find anything give me a yell." He stepped forward, then turned as the pilot made no motion to follow. "Are you going to leave this all to me?"

"No," said Faine reluctantly. His machete made a whistling sound as he swung it through the air. "I guess not."

The houses were of rough stone held together with a plaster of sandy mud, roofed with the twisted stems of the osphage and thatched with leaves. Most of the roofs were in need of repair and shafts of sunlight lit the interior rooms. The furniture was as primitive as the houses. Few walls bore any attempt at decoration. Stone lamps burning vegetable oil were the only visible means of illumination. The houses were better than caves but only just.

All were empty.

"Not a sign of life." Faine shook his head, baffled. "I don't understand it. Not a corpse, not a message, nothing. But the whole damned village is deserted." He stood, brooding then, "Could they have just up and left? Had a gutful, maybe, and just walked away?"

"Where to?"

"To another settlement? There's one beyond Major Peak, about fifteen miles east. There's another to the south about twenty. Or they could have decided to find a better place."

"Leaving everything behind?" Dumarest looked at the silent houses. "No," he said. "That isn't the answer. People don't walk off and leave everything behind. Not if they can help it." He led the way back to the landing field and stood looking at the ground. Faine followed his eyes.

"Hey," said the pilot. "The ground is all churned up. It looks as if quite a party landed here." He stooped, touching the dirt. "Fused. Rockets did that." Automatically he looked upward. "From space," he said. "Slavers, maybe?"

"It's possible."

"Well," said Faine, "What next?" He looked at Dumarest. "But would they have taken them all? There were some pretty old characters in the village. Would slavers have bothered to take them?"

"Why not?" Dumarest kicked at the dirt. "It stopped them from talking." He made his decision. "The friend I was looking for," he said. "His name was King. Caleb King. Do you know which was his house?"

"Old Caleb? Sure I do." Faine pointed the machete.

"It's the last one on the left past the community house. The one with the sign over the door." He shook his head. "Poor old Caleb. He told me once the sign was to bring good luck. Some luck!"

The house was as the others, mud-bound stone with a sagging roof and a dirt floor. There was only the one room. A cot with a thin, rumpled cover stood in one corner, a table and two chairs in the center. A row of wooden pegs supported clothing; a stove stood beside a scanty stock of fuel. Shelves bearing various utensils and items of personal use reared to either side of the door. A chest, open, stood at the foot of the bed.

Dumarest crossed the room and examined it. It contained a mess of clothing and nothing else. He straightened and stood frowning, trying to fit a face to the name of the man who had lived here.

He was old; that was the only thing of which he could be certain. The rest was nothing but rumor, a word caught in the lounge of a ship—a scrap of gossip enlarged to wile away an idle hour. A man, so the speaker had insisted, who claimed to have knowledge of legendary Earth. A joke, of course; what else could it be? Something to hear, laugh at and forget. Dumarest had not forgotten.

But he had arrived too late.

He stepped forward, leaning across the bed, searching the far side. He found nothing but, as he shifted his weight, his foot hit something beneath the cot. Lifting it he threw it to one side. A wooden trap showed against the dirt. He gripped the handle, heaved, heaved again, the veins standing out on his forehead. Something snapped and the trap flew open. Freshly broken wood showed against one edge. He had burst the crude lock in his impatience.

A short flight of steps led down to a cellar six feet

high and ten square. Stopping, he tried to examine it by
the diffused light from above. It wasn't enough. Returning upstairs he found and lit a stone lamp. The wick
smoked and the oil stank but it did its job. The cellar
was lined with jars of sun-baked mud from which rose
the sickly sweet smell of fermenting honey. *The old
man's wine vault,* he thought; *but why hide it down
here?*

The answer came as he returned above. Already the
sun was striking with naked fury and turning the inside
of the house into an oven. Yeast could not live in such
temperatures. The cellar was nothing more than a
means to provide a suitable environment for the living
cells.

Disappointed, Dumarest closed the trap and stepped
toward the door. A ray of sunlight shone from a scrap of
polished metal and illuminated a patch beside the door.
Scratched on a big stone, ragged as if done in haste, out
out of proportion as if drawn by night, was a peculiar
design. Dumarest recognized it at once.

The Cyclan seal.

Faine was nowhere in sight when he left the house.
Dumarest walked quickly toward the landing field,
relaxing as he saw the machine. He saw the pilot as he
reached the flitter; the man was standing at the edge of
the rows of osphage. As Dumarest watched Faine
swung his arm, the sunshine splintering from the
machete, and a huge bloom fell to the ground. Faine
stabbed it with the tip of the big knife, lifted it to his
shoulder and carried it back to the field. He grinned as
he saw Dumarest.

"Just getting us some breakfast," he explained. He
threw the severed bloom to the ground. "This one's
about ripe for eating." With the machete he lopped off

the fringe of petals and exposed the interior of the flower. A few bright green insects were trapped in a nest of fiber. "They crawl in to feed," said the pilot. "At night the blooms smell like fury. These things get attracted. They climb in and get knocked out by the perfume." He cut off the entire upper section. "I suppose it's a case of the would-be biter getting bitten." He wielded the blade again and handed Dumarest a section of thick, juicy pulp. "Go ahead," he urged. "It's good."

It tasted like peach, like grape, like tangy orange. The consistency was that of a melon. It quenched the thirst and satisfied the stomach though the nourishment value was probably low.

"The bees eat it all the time," said Faine, cutting himself another slice. "The settlers, anyone who can get it. For humans it has to be just ripe or it tastes like dirt and eats like leather. Two days," he added. "That's the maximum. Too early and it's raw. Too late and it's rotten. Like some more?"

Dumarest ate, his eyes thoughtful. "Tell me," he said. "Old Caleb, did you know him well?"

"As well as you can ever know anyone in the Freelands." Faine looked at his hands. They were sticky with juice. He wiped them on the front of his coverall. "Why?"

"Did he talk to you at all? About his past, I mean. Or did he always live here?"

"No. He arrived some while back. Never said very much but my guess is that he'd done his share of traveling. That's why I asked," he said. "I thought you two may have met up somewhere in the past."

"We'd never met," said Dumarest. He picked up a handful of dirt and rubbed it between his fingers to cleanse his hands of juice. "Has anyone ever come looking for him? Old friends, perhaps?''

''Not that I know of.'' Faine looked at the deserted village. ''You finished here?''

Dumarest glanced at the sky. The sun was approaching zenith; the search had taken longer than he'd thought. ''I'm finished,'' he said. ''We may as well go back now.'' He watched as the pilot walked to the flitter, opened the cabin door, rummaged inside to appear with an empty sack. He threw it over one shoulder and began to walk away. ''Where are you going?''

''Just to collect a few blooms.'' Faine was apologetic. ''The wife's fond of them and I like to get her some when I've got the chance.'' He jerked his head toward the empty houses. ''I don't reckon anyone will object.''

''No,'' said Dumarest. ''I suppose not.''

''I won't be long.'' Faine gestured with the machete and walked toward the osphage. Dumarest sat on the edge of the open door.

It had been another wasted journey. More time and money spent on a fruitless search for someone who might have concrete knowledge of the whereabouts of Earth. The planet existed, that he knew, but just where it rested in the galaxy was something impossible to discover. Almost impossible, he reminded himself. The information existed—it was only a matter of finding it.

He stretched, feeling the heat of the sun as it beat on his unprotected head and hands, the tough shirt, pants and boots that covered his body. The sun was too bright. It reflected from the ground in countless sparkles and shimmers as if the gritty soil held a high proportion of silicates. He raised his head and stared at the village. The sheds contained primitive canning equipment. The community house held a small infirmary, a recreation area and a place where, he supposed, people could worship. That, perhaps, was the reason for the bell.

An odd life, he thought. Harvesting the osphage as it ripened, stripping the husk from the small, valuable core, cutting, canning, sterilizing and sealing that core for later consumption. And living on the husks for fuel, the stems for building materials, the fiber for clothing. A hard, rough, precarious life based on a precarious economy. But, for these people, it was over.

Now, if Faine had been correct in his assumption, they were either dead or slaves.

It was possible. Slavers had been known to work that way. Dropping from the sky, sleep-gassing an entire community, taking their pick of salable human flesh and vanishing as quietly as they had come. But here? With labor so plentiful and cheap? Somehow he doubted it. Doubted too that any slaver would have taken an entire population, no matter how small. There were cheaper ways of closing a man's mouth than taking him up into space.

He stretched again, then tensed as something made an ugly tearing noise in the air. He rose and heard it again, catching a flashing glimpse of something red. It came a third time and he managed to follow it with his eyes. He looked behind and was halfway into the flitter, the door swinging shut, when he remembered Faine.

The man was deep among the osphage critically examining a freshly cut bloom. The blade of his machete was wet with juice, the sack at his feet bulging with stripped cores.

"Faine!" Dumarest shouted at the top of his voice. "Faine! Get back here! Fast!"

The pilot looked up.

"Quick, you fool! Run!"

Faine looked at Dumarest, looked past him, dropped the bloom and raced back through the osphage to the flitter. He reached Dumarest, passed him, eyes bright with terror, breath a wheezing rasp. A few yards from the machine he tripped and fell, the machete flying from his hand.

Dumarest snatched it up as the swarm arrived.

They came with a vicious hum of wings, large as sparrows, red as flame. Huge, mutated bees with stings curved like sabers, mandibles capable of shearing through tanned leather. Within seconds they filled the sky. Among them Dumarest fought for his life.

He felt a blow against his shoulder. Another in the region of his kidneys. Two more against his chest. The tough, spunmetal fabric of his clothing was proof against bite and sting. He ducked as slender legs trained across his face, lashing out with the machete, trying to clear the immediate area around his head. The blade was too long, too awkward. He dropped it and stiffened his hands, chopping with the edges, weaving, crouching, splintering red chitin as he dashed insects from the air.

Their size was against them. Had they been smaller neither man would have stood a chance. But they were big, heavy. They needed air-space and room to maneuver. Only a relative few could attack at a time and those few had a more enticing target than Dumarest.

Faine yelled as a cloud of bees settled on his juice-stained coverall. He beat at them, screaming when others settled on his head. Staggering, he threshed about, a living column of crawling red, helpless to defend himself. Dumarest realized with sick horror that the bees were literally eating the man alive.

He lunged forward, grabbed the pilot, smashed him hard against his chest. Crushed insects fell to the ground. He beat at the rest, knocking them from the man's head, then turned and lunged toward the open door of the flitter. The pilot screamed as Dumarest threw him into the cabin, screamed again as he was rolled onto the passenger seat. Dumarest slammed the door and punched viciously at the bees trapped inside. When the last had fallen he looked at the other man.

Faine was in a bad way. His face was horribly swollen, bloated so that the eyes were hidden behind folds of tissue, a thin liquid oozed between the folds. The flesh of his face, neck and upper chest was a mass of torn and bleeding wounds. His hands were puffed monstrosities. The pilot had been bitten and stung to the point of death.

Dumarest looked around. In the mess of the cabin he could see nothing resembling a first aid kit. He tore open a locker and threw an instruction manual to one side. A box yielded nothing but a few tools. Beside him Faine twitched and made little mewing sounds.

"Where is it?" yelled Dumarest. "The medical kit—where do you keep it?"

It was a waste of time. If Faine could hear he couldn't answer, not with his throat in the condition it was. And yet he was trying to talk. It took no imagination to realize what he was saying. A man in his hell of pain would have only one thought.

Dumarest hesitated. He could depress the carotid arteries and so cut off the blood supply to the brain. That would bring swift unconsciousness but, with the insect poison circulating in the bloodstream, it could be dangerous. And yet he had no choice. The flesh of face and head was so puffed it would be impossible to deliver an effective blow.

With the pilot released from pain Dumarest stared at the controls. The machine was primitive and the instruments unfamiliar, but he had watched Faine and

knew what to do. The engine started with a roar. The
down-blast from the rotors drove the crawling mass of
bees from the canopy so that he could see outside. The
swarm was busy among the osphage. Perhaps the bell
on the community house was to give warning so that the
villagers could get under cover. Or perhaps this had
been a rogue swarm looking for a nest.

If so, it had found one now. The village offered
plenty.

The rotors spun faster as Dumarest cautiously operated the controls. The flitter jerked and finally lifted,
creaking as Dumarest sent it up and away from the
village. He searched the horizon looking for the squat
tower of Major Peak. Faine had said there was a settlement five miles beyond. They would have an infirmary
and facilities for treating the pilot. Unless he received
correct attention he would die.

On his second swing around the village Dumarest
located the peak and sent the flitter droning toward it.
The machine was erratic. It demanded his total concentration. Thermals rising from the desert sent it slipping,
juddering, the rotors complaining as they churned the
air. But it flew, and that was all that mattered.

Back in the cabin something stirred. As large as a
sparrow, red as flame, it lifted its broken body and
spread undamaged wings. It was hurt, dying, but instinct drove it against its enemy. The hum of its wings
was lost in the roar of the engine. It landed on the back
of Dumarest's neck.

He felt it, guessed what it was, slapped frantically at
the insect. He felt it squash beneath his fingers but the
damage had been done. Pain, like a searing river of
boiling acid, flowed from where the sting had bitten
close to his spine. For a moment the world turned red
with agony.

A moment, but it was enough. The flitter was close to Major Peak, unsteady in the rising thermals. It yawed as Dumarest lost control, yawed again as he fought to regain it. A rotor, already weak, snapped beneath the strain. Like a crippled bird the flitter plummeted to the rocky base of the peak.

Dumarest released the controls, crouched, his body a ball and every muscle relaxed. He wedged himself tight between the seat and the instrument panel. The flitter hit, bounced, skittered down the slope to roll at the bottom. It slewed as it hit a boulder, the canopy shattering into a million crystalline shards. The air reeked with an acrid odor.

Dumarest smelled it as he staggered to his feet. He stooped, grabbed Faine by the collar and dragged the man from the wreckage. He had gone only a few yards when the crude distillate used as fuel hit the hot exhaust. He saw the flash, felt a giant hand thrust him forward and down, heard the sullen roar of expanding gases.

He twisted and looked back at the flitter. It was a mass of smoking flame, thick ashes drifting from the leaping column and falling like flakes of dirty gray snow. The pilot lay to one side. Dumarest crawled toward him, turned him over. A scrap of jagged metal was buried in his skull.

For Faine, at least, all troubles were over.

VII

DUMAREST woke shivering. For a moment he thought that he was traveling Low, the induction coils yet to warm his body, the lid still to rise and show him the handler with his steaming cup of Basic. Even the glare before his eyes seemed to be the diffused light of ultra-violet tubes in the cold-region of a ship. Then he blinked and the glare became stars as bright and as silver as a woman's hair. A very special woman. "Derai," said Dumarest. "Derai!" It was another illusion. The stars were stars, not hair. The ground was stony dirt, not the pneumatic mattress of a ship. He turned and saw a man sitting beside him, the starlight pale on his face.

"So you're awake," said Sar Eldon. "How do you feel?"

Dumarest sat upright before answering. He felt bruised, a little light-headed and had a raging thirst. He said so and the gambler laughed.

"I guess you would have. Hungry too, I bet. Right?"

"Right."

"We'll take care of that later," said Eldon. "Here's some water." He held the canteen as Dumarest drank. "How else do you feel?"

"I'm all right," said Dumarest. He looked to where a group of men sat around a smokeless fire. A cooking stove, he assumed, from the odor that wafted to his nostrils. "How did I get here?"

"We found you. We saw smoke and decided to investigate. You were in a pretty bad way. You'd been stung and in a bad place. An inch to the left, smack in the spine, and you'd be dead for sure. You'd also been eating osphage at night. The stuff's a narcotic then and it can be nasty. You were lucky."

Dumarest nodded, remembering.

"What happened?" asked the gambler curiously. "Did you upset someone and get yourself dumped? It's a habit some of the young bucks have," he explained. "One they're fond of. They think it's amusing. They take someone they don't like and dump him in the Freelands. If the bees don't get him then something else will. As it almost got you," he pointed out. "It's taken two days to get you back into shape."

"Two days? Here?"

"That's right." Sar locked his hands around his knees and leaned back, looking at the sky. "Want to tell me what happened?"

Dumarest told him. The gambler whistled. "Luck," he said. "Bad all the way."

"No," said Dumarest. "I wouldn't say that. Your finding me wasn't bad luck. Not for me." He reached for the canteen. "And you? What are you doing out here?"

"Working." Eldon paused as Dumarest drank. "Taking a chance so as to get a stake big enough to leave this lousy planet. You're in for a share of what we get."

"Why me?"

"If it hadn't been for you we'd all be starving back at the field. That or we'd have sold ourselves for a chance to make some profit too. Big profit."

Dumarest waited.

"Have you learned anything of the economy of this

world?'' Eldon waited for an answer. ''They produce
only one thing of real value. They call it ambrosaira—
it's the royal jelly of the mutated bees. Normally they
harvest it from their own hives; that's what the Hausi
wanted, labor for the job, but some bees aren't owned
by any House. They are the ones in the Freelands.
Wild, swarming when and where they will, nesting all
over the place. Dangerous too.''

''I've met them,'' reminded Dumarest. ''Have
you?''

''No.''

''Have any of the others?''

''We've got one man who's worked on a normal
harvest. This was his idea and he knows what to do.''
Sar turned, his face eager. ''Listen,'' he demanded.
''Do you know the value of that stuff? Traders load
themselves with rubbish just to get a little of it. All we
have to do is to find a nest, gas it, cut it open and help
ourselves.''

''Simple,'' agreed Dumarest. He thought of Faine.
''If it's so simple why aren't others doing it? Why
should they leave so much loot lying around?''

''The Houses,'' said Eldon quickly. ''They don't
like anyone but themselves gathering ambrosaira. They
want to keep a monopoly.''

''Then why don't they go after it as a team?''
Dumarest frowned, thinking. ''There's something
wrong here,'' he said. ''It can't be as simple as you
make out. Just what is the catch? Who put you up to
this, anyway?''

''I told you. We have a man with us who's worked on
other harvests.''

''Did he have money to back you?''

Eldon didn't answer.

"Someone must have," insisted Dumarest. "You didn't have money for equipment and transportation when you left the field. None of you did. So someone must have staked you. Who is it? The Hausi?"

"He supplied the equipment," admitted the gambler. "The transportation too. He'll come out for us when we signal. But he isn't going to buy the jelly."

"Who, then?"

"A trader. Scuto Dakarti. He'll buy all the jelly we can deliver. Cash down and no questions."

"And no responsibility either," pointed out Dumarest. "I suppose he told you how simple it all is. He or the agent. Who pays for the equipment if you don't find anything?"

"Does it matter?" The gambler rose to his feet. "We had no choice," he said quietly. "So they're cheating us. I know it, we all know it, but what can we do? If we find the jelly it won't matter. If we don't then we just owe more money. That," he added, "is why we'd like you to work with us. A double share if you do."

Dumarest hesitated.

"Think about it," said the gambler quickly. "Now let's eat." He led the way to the cooking stove. Someone passed up a plate filled with stew. Eldon handed it to Dumarest, accepted another, sat a little to one side. Both men ate with the concentration of those who are never certain as to when they will eat again. "That swarm," said Eldon. "The one you told me about. Do you think it settled?"

"It could have. The village was empty and Faine said they liked to find something hollow to use as a nest." Dumarest looked at his empty plate. "But I'm not going to guide you there. It wouldn't be any use," he explained. "We need an established nest with an established queen and a good stock of jelly.''

"That makes sense," said Eldon. "When do we start looking?"

Dumarest held out his plate for more food. "Later," he said. "When it's light.''

From the balcony the square looked very small, the figures of marching men even smaller. *Like ants,* thought Emil. *Like the little green scavenger beetles that take care of the refuse of Hive.* Their tunics helped the comparison. Green and silver, they marched and countermarched, going through exercises which had long lost all meaning, learning lessons for a war which could never be fought.

And each, thought Emil, *costing money.* A lot of money.

"They march well, my lord." Beside Emil the cyber stood tall in his scarlet robe, a splash of living color against the timeworn stone.

"They should." Emil was curt. "They have little else to do." He turned, vaguely conscious of the thin shouts of command rising from the square, the neat, mechanical movements of the men at their drill. Regor should appreciate their discipline, he thought. He, a living machine, would have an affinity with the automatons below. He said so. Regor demurred.

"No, my lord. Motion without purpose is a waste and unthinking obedience to empty commands is stupid. The Cyclan has no time for either.''

"You think this is stupid?" Emil gestured to the men in the square below.

"I think it unwise when the men could be better employed elsewhere. The percentage of total income necessary to maintain these men in idleness is far beyond all reasonable proportion. They are a burden, my lord, which is weakening your House.''

"So I should disband them?" Emil glared his contempt. "Leave Caldor unarmed and defenseless against
her enemies? Is that what you call good advice?"

"I am dealing with facts, my lord, not advice. Each
of those men has to be fed, housed, educated, clothed,
provided with recreation and medical attention. In return they give you what? An empty show of hollow
power. You cannot go to war because of the Pact. Why
then maintain an army?"

Sense, thought Emil. *Cold, emotionless logic. Trust
a cyber to give you that. What could such a man know of
pride and tradition? And yet he was right in what he
said: The House was too big and the land did not
expand with the family. But the alternative?*

"Give the head of each household a plot of land to
farm or to develop as he will," said Regor evenly. "Let
each person provide for himself. In return they will pay
you a ground rent for use of the land. This will assure
Caldor an income. Freed from the necessity of providing for all you can concentrate on politics. House-
loyalty will ensure that you are elected to a free parlia-
ment. Once in government you will have real power.
Power without responsibility."

But no men, no land, no dagger of rank swinging at
his belt, no men and women ready to touch a forelock or
curtsy as he passed. Instead he would be a politician
begging for votes. Begging from the very people over
whom he now held the power of life and death!

"No," said Emil. "There must be a different way.
Have you discovered anything in your researches?"

"Very little, my lord." Regor hesitated. "There is
one odd discrepancy. It concerns the rule of your—
father."

"The Old Man?" Emil frowned. "What about
him?"

"I have been checking past accounts, my lord. You

will remember that you ordered such a search in the hope of finding something which might be of advantage. During the time of the actual rule of the present Head of the House a certain percentage of income appears to have mysteriously vanished.''

"Stolen?" Emil glared at the cyber. "Dare you accuse him of theft?"

"I make no accusation, my lord. But the facts are undeniable. Fifteen percent of the total income was diverted into an unspecified account.''

Fifteen percent! Emil grew excited as he thought about it. The Old Man had actively ruled for almost a hundred years. Fifteen years' total income. Money enough to buy arms, hire mercenaries, bribe enemies, seduce friends. A fortune which, if wisely spent, could make Caldor the sole ruling House on Hive!

If he were permitted to use it.

If Johan, the actual successor, would allow it to be spent.

And, above all, if the Old Man, the only one who knew where it was, could be persuaded to divulge his secret.

The Old Man, who had not been able to communicate for years!

Dumarest crouched, watching. Ahead in a slight valley something gray and rounded rose above the gritty soil. It looked like a boulder, of which there were dozens in the vicinity. The camouflage, he thought, was superb.

"That?" Olaf Helgar, the man who'd had experience in harvesting the royal jelly, scowled and shook his head. "That's no hive."

"What did you expect?" Dumarest kept his voice

low, his body hidden. "A nice, sharp, regular structure? Even I know that wild bees make their nest to suit
themselves. Now watch! That opening under the slight
overhang. That's the entrance."

He froze as a scarlet bee hummed from somewhere
behind, hovered, landed and moved in the rhythmic
pattern of its message "dance." The drone of others
making for where it had signaled sounded like the
distant buzzing of a flitter.

"How do we go about it?" whispered Eldon. The
gambler looked pale but determined.

Helgar cleared his throat and swallowed. "We set up
nets," he said. "That's how they did it back on the
House-farm. A covering of nets so that the bees outside
can't get in. Then we gas the hive and stun those that are
inside. Then we dig in until we find the jelly." He
coughed again. "I guess the same procedure will work
here."

"What do you think, Earl?" Eldon turned to
Dumarest for confirmation.

"We'll need strong nets," said Dumarest. "And
what about masks?"

"We've got them."

"Pick out a team to work inside the nets. Helgar and
some others. Make sure that everyone is well covered.
Pad out all you can and don't leave an inch of skin
unprotected." Dumarest looked at the sky. It seemed
clear. "Have you any weapons?" Eldon shook his
head. "What about the cooking stove? Can it be
adapted?"

"I guess so," said the gambler slowly. "What's on
your mind, Earl?"

"I've seen a wild swarm," said Dumarest. "I know
what it's like. Ordinary nets aren't going to stand up for

long. We need something outside to keep them away.
Something like a flamethrower. Maybe I can make one
out of the stove.''

He examined it as the others got ready. The burner
was fed from a tank of compressed gas. The valve was
adjustable. He worked at it until the tank was free of its
casing yet still attached to the burner feed-pipe. A scrap
of sponge platinum acted as an igniter, the catalyst
firing the gas on contact. He turned the valve and a
long, thin jet of flame streaked upward. Picking up a
stone Dumarest carefully hammered at the nozzle.
When he tried again the flame spread into a wide fan.
Satisfied, he laid aside the crude weapon.

Eldon came over from where the men were checking
each other's equipment. He looked grotesque in his
layers of assorted clothing. His face, beneath the up-
lifted mask, was streaming with perspiration. He
handed Dumarest a mask. "This is a spare," he said.
"You'd better put it on."

Dumarest adjusted the clumsy mesh and fabric res-
pirator.

"We're all ready to go," said the gambler. He
sounded nervous. "I guess we'll be safe enough. Olaf
thinks so, anyway, and he should know."

"That's right," said Dumarest. "He should." He
looked to where the man was busy assembling his nets.
Now that he was working at something familiar the man
had gained confidence.

"All right," Olaf said. "This is how we work it.
Those I've picked will come with me. As soon as we
reach the hive the others will throw up the nets. Leave
that to them and don't worry about it. Those without gas
tanks will block every opening they can find. While
they're at it the rest of us will be busy feeding in the gas.

When I give the word we start digging. Leave collect-
ing the jelly to me. Any questions?''

"What happens if the bees rush us?''

"Ignore them. The gas will get them soon enough.
All ready?'' Helgar lowered his mask. "Let's go.''

Dumarest stood back, watching as the others
worked. Aside from an initial fumbling they worked
smoothly enough, the nets rising to make a rough
hemisphere about the nest and the men inside. Eldon
came back to join him where he stood.

"That's it,'' he said. "There's nothing we can do
now but wait.''

"There's one thing,'' said Dumarest. He flexed his
hands inside the tough gauntlets the gambler had given
him. "You can send for the flitter. Get it out here fast.''

"Before we've got the jelly?''

"That's right.'' Dumarest threw back his head, staring again at the sky, narrowing his eyes against the
glare of the sun. "It'll take time to get here,'' he
explained. "We might be lucky, in which case it can
wait. But get it here just in case.''

Eldon was anxious. "You expect trouble?''

"Not exactly,'' said Dumarest. "But let's not take
chances. We may have to leave here in a hurry.'' He
turned as Eldon busied himself with the portable radio,
watching the men inside the nets. Helgar had them well
organized. Gas plumed from nozzles clamped to the
openings of the hive. As he watched a small cluster of
bees darted from an overlooked opening. Olaf turned
his nozzle toward them, sending them to the ground.
Others trod them into the dirt.

Again Dumarest searched the sky.

"What are you looking for?'' Eldon put away the
radio. "This is easy,'' he said, not waiting for an

answer, entranced by the men at work. "Dead easy. We should really be able to clean up while we're at it."

"Maybe." Dumarest wasn't convinced. "Look around," he said. "Find somewhere we can hide if we have to. A place the bees can't get at us. A small cave which can be blocked, something like that." He went across to where the other men outside the nets stood watching the men at work. "Get something to hit with," he ordered. "Something strong to use as a weapon. And find where you can make a stand if you have to." They hesitated, reluctant to move. "Do it!" he snapped. "Those men in there are relying on us to protect them. Move!"

Inside the nets the men were hard at work. Dirt showered as they dug into the hive, exposing a mass of honeycomb and gassed bees. Red mixed with gray as the debris mounted. The yellow of sticky honey fouled tools and boots. Suddenly Helgar yelled an order.

"All right," he said. "Take it easy now. Leave this part to me."

They stepped back as he set to work. Outside the nets the others craned forward, forgetting Dumarest's orders, eager to see what they had gained. Dumarest caught Eldon, held him back. "Stay here."

"But I want to see."

"Stay here, you fool!"

"No." The gambler jerked his arm free. "I want to see what we've found," he said stubbornly. "I've got to take a look."

He moved away and Dumarest let him go. He had done what he could. Again he looked at the sky, cradling the improvised flamethrower in his arms. The mask was hot, stifling, but he did not remove it. Not then and not minutes later when the sky suddenly turned red with bees.

VIII

THE OFFICE was just the same. The same desk, the chairs, the map pinned to the wall—an unpretentious facade for a man who was far richer than he wanted others to think. A part of the regular stock-in-trade of a Hausi. Yamay Mbombo looked up from his desk as Dunarest entered the room. "So you're back," he said. "The others?"

"Dead."

"All of them?"

"Every last one." Tiredly Dumarest sank into a chair. His clothes were soiled, fretted as if by the teeth of a gigantic saw, the spun-metal gleaming through the plastic covering. "Faine too. His flitter got burned. You may as well pay his wife the deposit. I shan't argue about it."

"But I may." The agent leaned forward with a sudden flash of teeth, white against the ebony of his skin. "You traveled back at my expense," he pointed out. "And you had a little trouble with my pilot."

"He wasn't expecting me," said Dumarest. "He didn't seem to want to give me a lift. I had to persuade him to change his mind."

"He told me," said Yamay. "On the radio after you'd left him. He had the idea that you would have killed him if he'd refused."

"Yes," said Dumarest. "I probably would. Just as

you killed those poor devils you sent out to hunt for your jelly."

The agent was quick to protest. "Not mine! Scuto Dakarti put them up to it."

"And you equipped them. Knowing all the time they didn't stand a chance of getting away with it."

"It was a gamble," admitted Hausi. "But Eldon was a gambler. He knew the odds were against him. How could I refuse if he was willing?" He hesitated. "Was it bad?"

"Bad enough." Dumarest didn't want to talk about it. The bees had come as he had sensed they would. They had settled, literally burying the others beneath the weight of their bodies. Thousands of them. Millions. Covering every inch of ground in a heaving mass of red. He had managed to burn his way clear, running because he'd had no choice, finally managing to find cover where he had waited until the flitter had arrived. "You should have warned them," he said. "The bees in the Freelands are telepathic. Somehow those in the nest radiated a signal for help."

"I didn't know," said the agent. "How could I have known! Telepathic," he said. "Are you sure about that?"

"How else could they have arrived at the critical time?" demanded Dumarest. "And they didn't belong to the hive we attacked. There were too many of them for that. Somehow they learned of the danger and combined against it. If that isn't telepathy then it's something pretty close to it."

"It is possible," admitted the agent. "On this planet most things are." Again he hesitated. "I take it that you had no luck? You have no jelly?"

"No."

The agent sat for a moment, thinking, then he shrugged. "Well, we cannot win every time and this time we all lose. Faine his life and flitter. Eldon and his friends their lives. Scuto his jelly. I lose my equipment and you lose your deposit."

"Which," reminded Dumarest pointedly, "goes to Faine's widow."

"She will get it," said the agent. "That I promise and I am a man of my word." It was true enough. A Hausi did not lie, though he might not tell all of the truth. "And now let me offer you a drink."

Dumarest sipped, his stomach uneasy at the taste of honey, but the alcohol warmed some of his fatigue. The agent refilled his glass. "Your friend," he said. "The one you were looking for. Did you find him?"

"No."

"Was he not at the village?"

"It was deserted. Faine thought that slavers might have been at work."

"On Hive?"

"That's what I thought. It doesn't seem reasonable." Dumarest set down his glass. "I've wondered about that," he said. "I've also wondered why it was necessary for us to allow others to reach there ahead of us."

"To raid the village?" The agent shook his head. "I doubt it. What possible reason could anyone have for doing such a thing?" He sipped his wine, smiling. "I can think of a far simpler explanation. Faine had a liking for osphage. It cannot be collected at night. It was his custom, when going into the Freelands, to collect a few cores for sale in the market. He probably did not want to waste the opportunity of earning some extra money."

"I expect you're right." Dumarest picked up his glass and slowly emptied it. "Are there any cybers on Hive?"

"The House of Caldor has one. There could be others but I doubt it. The services of the Cyclan do not come cheap." Yamay reached for the bottle. "Someone was inquiring after you," he said. "A person I think that you would be very eager to meet."

"Derai?"

The agent's smile told Dumarest how he had betrayed himself. "The girl? No. Her half-brother. His name is Blaine. He is waiting at the Tavern of the Seven Stars." His smile grew still wider as Dumarest made no effort to move. "I think you should meet him but first another drink, a bath and a change of clothes." Steadily he poured the wine. "It would not be wise to make a bad impression."

The tavern was a long, low, timber-roofed affair with paneled walls on which hung dusty trophies of forgotten hunts. Thick plank tables and pegged chairs filled the main area. A raised dais at one end provided space for musicians and entertainers. The floor was of polished wood and the place shone with the gleam of pewter, copper and brass.

Blaine joined Dumarest as he sat and ordered a flask of wine. "You will pardon me," he said apologetically. "The vintage you have ordered is not of the best. A flagon of Caldor Supreme," he said to the serving wench. "Chilled but not too cold."

"At once, my lord."

Over the wine Dumarest studied his host. Young, he decided, and a little spoiled. Cynical too by the lines around his mouth and more than a little bitter. A man who has been forced to accept what he does not like someone who has learned to tolerate what he cannot change. But noble. The dagger at his belt showed that. And of the same House as Derai. The green and silver were unmistakable.

"I am Derai's half-brother," said Blaine. "She asked me to meet you. There are things she would like you to understand."

Dumarest poured more wine.

"Do you know what she is?" Blaine stared at Dumarest over the rim of his glass. "Do you?"

Dumarest was curt. "I know."

"Then you should be able to appreciate her reason for acting as she did. At the gate, when she walked away from you, can you guess why she did that?"

"The journey was over. My job was done."

"And you thought she had no further need of you?" Blaine shook his head. "If you believe that then you are a fool and I do not take you for that. The man who met her is her cousin. His name is Ustar and he fully intends making her his wife. He is also of a savage nature and prides himself on his skill with a dagger. Had he guessed how she felt toward you he would have killed you where you stood. She walked away so as to save your life."

"It is possible," said Dumarest, "that I would have had something to say about that."

"Yes," said Blaine. "No doubt you would. But Ustar is a high member of an established House. Just how far do you think you would have got had you bested him? No, my friend, Derai did what had to be done." He drank and refilled his glass with the cool, osphage-flavored wine. "A strange person, my half-sister. We have a little in common. I can sense things which trouble her. Sometimes I can almost read her emotions. When they are very strong I can. She loves you," he said abruptly. "She needs you more than she has ever needed anyone else. That's why I'm here. To tell you that."

"You have told me," said Dumarest. "Now what am I supposed to do?"

"Wait. I have some money for you. Your money. Not all of it but as much as I could get." His voice reflected his bitterness. "Money isn't plentiful among the Caldors. Not when there are so many to be fed and housed. But live quietly until she sends for you. It may not be for long."

Wait, thought Dumarest bleakly. *Until a bored woman decides to relieve her boredom? No,* he told himself. *Not that. Wait, yes, for just as long as necessary to get a ship away from here.* And yet he knew that he wouldn't go. Not while he thought she needed him. Not while he wanted to be needed by her.

"You love her too," said Blaine suddenly. "You don't have to answer. She knows and that is good enough. You can't hide a thing like that from a telepath," he said. "You can't lie to Derai. That is one thing my dear cousin will never remember. He thinks that it will make no difference, but it will. She will never go willingly to his bed." He helped himself to more wine. He was more than a little drunk, Dumarest realized, but the alcohol had turned him into himself, made him talk of things normally left unsaid.

"A strange family, the Caldors," said Blaine. "My mother—well, never mind that. Derai? My father found her mother somewhere in the Freelands. It would account for her talent. Ustar? He's the legitimate one. Born of accepted parents but with the bad luck to be sired by the wrong father. He can't succeed to the control of the House. Neither can I, but Derai can. So you see why he wants to marry her?"

"Yes," said Dumarest. "I see." He refilled Blaine's glass. "You have a cyber attached to your House," he said. "Tell me about him."

"Regor? A fine man." Blaine drank a little of his wine. "I wanted to be a cyber once," he said. "I wanted it more than anything in my life. To be a part of something, accepted, respected, acknowledged by the highest. To be always self-assured and confident. To be able to take a handful of facts and, from them, to be able to predict the logical sequence of events. To be able, in a way, to foretell the future. To have power," he said. "Real power." He drank and brooded a little. "I applied for membership," he said. "I even went into initial training. They failed me. Can you guess why?"

"Tell me," said Dumarest.

"They said that I was emotionally unstable. Not good material for a cyber. Not even good enough to be accepted by one as a servant. A failure. That's what I've been all my life. A failure."

"No," said Dumarest. "You weren't a failure. To be turned down by the Cyclan isn't that."

"You don't like them?" Blaine looked at Dumarest, let his eyes fall to his hand. It was clenched tight around his glass. As Blaine watched, the crystal shattered.

"They take you," said Dumarest quietly, "very young and very impressionable. They teach you never to feel emotion and to gain pleasure only from mental achievement. And, just to make it simple for you to do this, they operate on the nerves leading to the brain. You didn't fail," he insisted. "You succeeded. You can taste and feel and know the meaning of pleasure and pain. You know what it is to laugh and cry and feel hate and fear. A cyber can do none of these things. He eats and drinks but the food and water is tasteless fuel for his body. He is incapable of love. He is a stranger to physical sensation. He can know only the pleasure of mental achievement. Would you change your life for that?''

Blaine sat thinking, remembering. ''No,'' he said at last. ''I don't think I would.''

''You mentioned Derai's mother,'' said Dumarest casually. ''You said that she came from the Freelands.''

''That's right.''

''The village she came from. Was it Lausary?''

''I don't know. Is it important?''

''No, forget it.'' Dumarest helped them both to more wine, using a glass from another table to replace the one he had broken. He was feeling the reaction to past activity. The invigorating effects of the bath Yamay had given him were almost totally absorbed by the fatigue, so that he had trouble keeping his eyes open. And memory was beginning to intrude.

He lifted his glass, drank, refilled it and drank again. Perhaps, if he drank enough, he would be able to forget the screams of Eldon and the others, the harsh stridulation of bees seared and burning in the flame, the desperate fear of being suffocated by the press of their bodies.

And running, running. It didn't help to know that he could have done nothing else.

He drank and thought of Derai, Derai, who loved him and who knew that he loved her. Derai!

He lowered his empty glass and saw Ustar.

He stood very straight, very proud, a disdainful expression on his face as his eyes searched the tavern. He was not alone. Three others wearing the green and silver stood at his back. Like dogs they followed him as he moved between the tables.

''Ustar!'' Blaine, suddenly cold sober, moved restlessly at Dumarest's side. ''He's looking for you.

You'd better go before he sees you.''

Dumarest picked up the near-empty bottle, emptied it into their glasses. "Why should he be looking for me?"

"I don't know," admitted Blaine. "But he's looking for trouble. Please go. Derai would never forgive me if anything happened to you."

"Finish your wine," said Dumarest, "and learn something: trouble does not vanish because you run away from it." He leaned back, watchful, the empty bottle close to hand. It was not an ideal weapon but, in a pinch, it would serve.

"Cousin!" Ustar had seen them. He strode forward, his companions at his heels. "Well, cousin," he sneered, "you certainly keep strange company."

Blaine took a sip of his wine. "Dumarest is my friend."

"Your friend?" Ustar raised his eyebrows. "A cheap traveler? A man who forced his unwanted attentions on your sister? Come, cousin, you cannot be serious."

"Has Derai complained about Dumarest?"

"That," said Ustar coldly, "is beside the point. I say he has insulted her. That is enough."

He made no attempt to lower his voice. A hush spread from the adjoining tables across the tavern as others grew aware of what was happening. Against the far walls men stood so as to get a better view. Dumarest recognized the tension in the air, the anticipation of blood. It was the same the universe over.

Blaine was defiant. "Derai is my sister. If she has been insulted I shall attend to it."

"You?" Ustar loaded the word with contempt. "You?"

"You're looking for trouble," said Blaine. He was

pale with anger. "Well, look elsewhere. Perhaps you can pick a fight with a ten year old boy. It should be a good match," he added, "if you tie one arm behind his back."

"Are you challenging me, cousin?"

"No," said Blaine. "I don't go for your games. Now just vanish and leave me alone."

"With the thing you call a friend?" Ustar looked at Dumarest for the first time. "Surely, cousin, the honor of our House is still something to be considered? Even," he added deliberately, "by a bastard like you."

Dumarest grabbed Blaine as he lunged across the table. "Hold it!" he snapped. "Can't you see that he's trying to goad you into acting the fool?"

"I'll kill him," said Blaine thickly. "One day I'll kill him."

"One day," agreed Dumarest. "But not now." He rose and looked at Ustar. "With your permission," he said flatly, "we will leave now."

"Filth! You will stay!"

"As you wish." Dumarest looked at Ustar, his friends, the watchful clients of the tavern. "For some reason that I do not know you wish to pick a fight with me. Is this correct?"

"You have insulted the Lady Derai," said Ustar. "The honor of my House demands that you be made to pay."

"With blood, naturally," said Dumarest dryly. "You will understand if I am reluctant to cooperate." Deliberately he moved from behind the table and passed the group of men. He heard the sharp intake of breath, the rustle of movement, and turned to see Ustar's dagger lunging at his chest. Almost too late he remembered that the clothes he wore were not his own. He caught the dagger wrist with his left hand, the smack of meeting flesh shockingly loud. The point of the weapon halted an inch from his blouse.

"Shame!" A man stood shouting from the side of the tavern. He wore a tunic of blue and gold. "By God, Ustar, I would never have believed it! A stab in the back!"

"He wears armor!" yelled one of Ustar's companions. "We could tell at once. Ustar knew that he couldn't hurt the man."

The lie went unchallenged. Those watching neither knew nor cared if it was true.

"Make it a fair fight!" A man wearing black and yellow called out from his position on top of a table. "Two to one on the stranger!"

"A fair fight," echoed others. "Make it a fair fight!"

Ustar thinned his lips. It was a free tavern owning allegiance to no House and he was unpopular with those watching. But still he was confident. "All right," he said. "But he'll have to strip to the waist."

On reflection he was glad things had turned out this way. Now he would be free of any taint of murder. Not that it worried him but it would help that Derai wouldn't be able to accuse him of that. Not with Blaine as an honest eyewitness.

"He's fast," said Blaine as helped Dumarest to strip. "Fond of coming in and up from low down." He pursed his lips as he saw the naked torso. It was blotched and marked with ugly bruises. The spun-metal had been proof against puncture but not against impact.

Dumarest sucked air deep into his lungs as the watchers made a ring in the center of the floor. He was tired and ached all over. His reflexes could not help but be slow and Ustar was an experienced fighter. It showed in his every move, but he had made no attempt

to strip and Dumarest wondered why such a man should
give him an apparent advantage.

"Here!" Blaine thrust his dagger into Dumarest's
hand. "Use this and good luck!"

Ustar came in quick, fast, giving no warning. His
blade shone in the light, a trap for the eyes, the glitter
dying as he twisted the steel. Dumarest parried with
conditioned reflex, feeling the jar against his hand as
the knives met, the shock up wrist and arm. Immediately Ustar sprang back, forward again, lips thinned into a killer's snarl, the blade rising in a vicious stab
from below. Again Dumarest parried, feeling the cold
burn of the edge as it touched his side. A hissing
inhalation from the crowd signaled the sight of blood.

Ustar laughed, a short bark of sound without humor,
and again attacked, blade lancing toward the groin.
Dumarest blocked, blocked again, then knew he dared
take no more chances. He was too tired, his opponent
too fast; the fight had to be ended and soon.

He fell back, lowering his guard, tempting Ustar to
attack. Again steel clashed as he parried the upward
thrust but this time he trapped the blade, turning it aside
from his body before slashing out with his own dagger,
the blade sweeping around and up toward the face.
Contemptuously Ustar stepped back and, too late, recognized the danger. Dumarest continued the attack,
giving the other man no time to regain his balance,
cutting savagely at the body. The blade bit home, the
edge sliced into the tunic and Dumarest felt the stubborn grate of metal.

Ustar was wearing a steel shirt beneath the green and
silver.

Immediately Dumarest attacked again, moving with
a savage burst of speed, throwing himself forward, his
blade a glitter of light as it stabbed at the eyes. Ustar fell

back, desperately parrying, his movements wide, his
face tense with fear. Finally he managed to gain time to
make a frenzied lunge at the body. Dumarest had expected it. As the knife and arm shot forward he weaved,
allowed it to pass between his side and left arm, dropping his left hand to trap the wrist. He twisted, forcing
Ustar to his knees, drawing back his right hand with the
dagger poised for the thrust.

"No!" Ustar stared at the implacable face above his
own. "For God's sake! No!"

The dagger moved forward, light splintering from
the point.

"Please!" screamed Ustar. His face was wet with
perspiration. "Please don't kill me!"

Dumarest hesitated, then, reversing the dagger,
smashed the heavy pommel between Ustar's eyes.

IX

THERE WAS, Derai told herself, nothing to be afraid of. It was just an old man in a bed. A very old man but that was all. And yet the fear remained. Never before had she seen the actual Head of the House. Grandfather had been a legendary figure, someone mentioned as still being alive but never seen. Now she was within the same room and about to meet him face to face.

"Are you ready, my lady?" Regor stood at her side, his shaven head skull-like against the scarlet of his thrown-back cowl. "It will not be a pleasant sight," he warned. "He is very old and very ill. Extreme age can sometimes distort the human frame." The cyber's hand was firm on her elbow as he led her toward the bed.

She stood looking, saying nothing, her eyes enormous against the pallor of her face.

"The ambrosaira which has extended his life has, in many ways, altered his metabolism," said Regor. He didn't bother to lower his voice; the thing in the bed could not hear. "It is almost as if it were trying to convert the flesh, bone and blood into another shape. An insect shape. But he is still human, my lady. It is important you remember that."

She nodded, clenching her hands, feeling the nails dig into her palms. It was hard not to scream. Not because of what she saw, though that was bad enough, but of what she mentally heard: the soundless, wordless, incoherent screaming that had too often driven her to the limits of sanity. Now she knew what it was: an old and terrified mind locked in an unresponsive prison of decaying flesh.

"You are the only one who can help him," said Johan quietly. He stood at the foot of the bed staring at his daughter. *She is,* he thought, *amazingly calm. We should have guessed before,* he told himself, *but we always assumed the Old Man was drugged and unconscious. But,* he reminded himself, *as Regor pointed out, the subconscious never sleeps.*

He felt a momentary anger instantly quelled. No one was to blame.

"You understand, my lady, what it is we are asking you to do?" Regor looked from the bed to the girl. "He cannot communicate, yet he holds knowledge we need to possess. You could gain it for us by reading his mind."

"I could," she admitted. "But only if he concentrates on germane matters. How are you going to ask him what it is you want to know?"

"I will attend to that, my lady." Trudo looked up from where he stood with his apparatus on the other side of the bed. Against one wall Emil leaned beside a window, able to do nothing but watch. It irritated him that he could do no more but, for now, everything was up to the girl.

"I do not know if what I have done will be successful," said the physician quietly. "As far as I can determine he is totally unresponsive to external stimuli. This may be because the sensory nerves have ceased to function or because the motor nerves governing response are paralyzed. You, I hope, will be able to tell us if I am making contact." He adjusted the apparatus at his side. "I have bypassed the aural organs and made direct electronic contact with the bone. It is possible that, with the use of sufficient power, he may hear what we have to say.'' He lifted a microphone and spoke gently into the instrument. "My lord, can you hear me?''

A pause. Derai shook her head.

Again the physician spoke. Again, again, each time increasing the power of his machine so that the equivalent decibel strength rose to that of a clap of thunder.

"Wait!'' Derai closed her eyes the better to concentrate. It came again, a question, a stirring in the vortex of nightmare. A desperate hope which was like a strained echo of sound.

"What is that? Who is speaking? Who is there?"

Trudo caught her signal, spoke again in the selected phrases which Regor had chosen, words devoid of ambiguity, compact in their message-to-noise ratio. Again she caught the seething echo, stronger now, blazing with hope—life struggling to survive.

"I can hear you! You must listen to me! You must help me . . . me . . . me. . ."

The words reverberated as if down empty corridors, a repeated echo of a mind which had suddenly become disjointed, intoxicated with euphoria. She felt it and shared it. Her eyes shone like stars.

Emil watched from his position beside the window. The useless hulk of flesh was at last being stirred to life. The Old Man who had been kept alive for reasons of tradition rather than affection would soon be forced to yield his precious secret. But why didn't she ask about the money? *The money, damn you! Ask about the money!* Anger, impatience, hate and a red tide of greed.

Johan moved restlessly where he stood. *If she shows signs of pain I'll stop it immediately. Stop it and to hell with Emil and his ambitions!* Concern and protective defiance.

Trudo adjusted his machine. *The skull must be al-most completely ossified to need such power to vibrate the bone. It would be interesting to dissect—but they would never allow it.* Regret and frustration.

The thoughts swirled like smoke, filling the room with mental noise, tearing at her concentration with conflicting emotion overriding, by sheer volume, the wisp of rational communication she was building with the grotesque horror on the bed.

Another thought, this time hard, clear, direct: *Order them from the room, my lady. I can work the machine.*

The cyber, recognizing the situation, predicting the logical outcome, advising the best thing to do.

Advice which she had no choice but to take.

"Impossible!" Emil rose from his chair, strode three paces, turned and walked back again. The room was at the foot of the tower in which the Old Man had his bedchamber. Once it had been a guard room and the furnishings were still spartan. "I don't believe it," snapped Emil. "The thing is preposterous!"

"I assure you, my lord, the Lady Derai is telling nothing but the truth." Against Emil's display the cyber's calm was enhanced. Johan cleared his throat.

"Let us be logical about this," he suggested. "We asked Derai to do something for us. She has done it. We now have to decide what action to take on the basis of her information. To deny that information is ridicu-lous." He looked at his daughter. "Derai?"

"I will tell you again," she said dully. Fatigue had marked her face with midnight shadows. "He wants to live. He will tell you what you want to know if you will guarantee his continued existence."

Put that way it sounded simple but there was no way she could tell them of the horrible lust for life still smoldering in the decaying flesh, the animal cunning, the incredible determination still to rule, still to be the actual Head of Caldor. There had been times when she had been almost physically ill. Others when only the cyber and his insistence had kept her beside the bed.

"That's what I mean," said Emil. Again he paced the floor. "The thing can't be done." He turned to face the physician. "Can it?"

"Not on Hive, my lord." Trudo pursed his lips. "And I doubt if there are any worlds on which it could be done. Not in his present condition. The state of his metabolism makes a brain-transplant impossible. Even a cybernetic hookup would lead to foreseeable complications. His blood is no longer what we regard as normal," he explained. "It would take too long to manufacture an artificial surrogate." He made a helpless gesture. "I am sorry, my lord. I cannot help you. I am of the opinion that what he demands cannot be done."

"As I said." Emil glowered at Derai. "Are you certain that you are telling the truth, girl? Did you dig down deep and find out what he really wanted? Or is this just some trick to explain your failure?"

"That will be enough!" Johan's voice held unaccustomed strength. "You forget yourself, Emil. I, not you, am the nominal Head of Caldor."

"For how long?" Emil glared his frustration. "Until mounting debts swallow what we have left? Listen to me, brother. If Caldor is to survive we need money. The Old Man has it. Enough to make our House the ruler of Hive." He looked at the cyber. "Is that not correct, Regor?"

"It is, my lord."

"So we have to win his secret." Emil stood, thinking. "But how? How?"

"By doing what he wants," said Derai. She looked at the cyber. "Tell them."

"There is another way to give him continued existence other than by actual physical longevity," explained Regor. "We can do it by supplying a subjective world of hallucination."

"Drugs?" Trudo was interested. "It could be done, I suppose, but—" He shook his head. "Not without some communication," he pointed out. "There has to be some medium for the relaying of hypnotic suggestion. It was a good idea, cyber," he said, condescendingly, "but it will not work."

"On Hive no," agreed Regor. "Our medical science and ability are far too primitive. But Hive is not the only planet in the universe. There is another. Folgone."

"Folgone?" Emil frowned. "I've never heard of it." He looked up at the ceiling. "Has he?"

"Yes, my lord. The suggestion came from himself. He is aware that, in his case, there is something far better than simple physical longevity. It is to be found on Folgone."

"You know of this world?" Johan was abrupt.

"Yes, my lord."

"Then it exists? It isn't just the sick fancy of a dying man?"

Regor was emphatic. "It is far from that, my lord. Folgone is the one place which can give him a thousand years of subjective hallucination so intense as to be superior to normal existence."

"A paradise," said Emil sourly. "I wonder that others aren't eager to share its pleasures."

"They are, my lord, make no mistake about that." Regor turned to face Johan. "It will not be easy to win a place. Few are offered and many strive. And there are other details which should be attended to. The journey is long and passage should be arranged. Perhaps a ship will have to be chartered. That is," he added, "if you intend doing as the patient demands."

Johan hesitated, thinking of the expense. Emil could think only of the promised reward.

"We'll do it," he said. "We have no choice." He caught sight of Johan's expression. "The Old Man is still the Head of the House," he pointed out. "It is his right to be taken where he will. It is our duty to obey."

Johan looked at his brother. "Your respect for duty does you credit," he said acidly. "But we have still to find means to do as you suggest. I am reluctant to risk the little we have. Duty to the House," he added, "comes before duty to the individual."

It was Emil's turn to hesitate. Money could be found—the trader had shown him how—but there were still complications. The city was full of ears and eyes, a hotbed of intrigue. If the rumor should circulate that he was selling undeclared jelly the reaction would be extreme. Caldor would be accused of violating the Pact. But, somehow, there had to be a way.

"Dumarest," said Derai, reading his mind. She smiled, suddenly no longer tired. "Dumarest," she said again. "Blaine will tell him what it is you want."

Emil scowled, thinking of Ustar, his terribly swollen eyes, his broken nose, hiding his pain and anger in a secluded room. Ustar, who had made himself appear a fool and worse. Dumarest had been the cause of that— the traveler who Derai so obviously loved. It would be insane to throw them even closer together.

Then, looking at her, he realized that he had no choice.

"No." Dumarest turned from the window he had been staring through. It was on the upper floor of a tavern which overlooked the field. Lights shone on the perimeter fence, gleaming from the hulls of the two ships standing on the gravel. Other lights shone from the streets and houses of the town. From the window it was possible to drop to the roof of a porch below and from there into the street. "No," he said again. "I'm sorry but I'm just not interested."

"But why not?" Blaine was bewildered. A refusal was the last response he had considered. He looked around the narrow room. It held a cot, a chair, a chest of drawers against a wall. The floor was bare. The light came from a lamp burning vegetable oil. The only thing it could have in its favor was that it was cheap.

"Look," he said urgently. "There's only the few of us. The Old Man, naturally; he has to go. Derai to read his mind. Emil won't be left out of it. I'm going to take care of Derai. And there's Regor," he added. "The cyber has to work the machine. The one used to talk to the Old Man."

Dumarest made no comment.

"You've got to come," said Blaine. "We need you. Derai needs you. She won't go if you refuse." He caught hold of Dumarest's arm. "Why do you refuse?"

Someone knocked on the door before Dumarest could answer. Yamay entered, a parcel beneath his arm. He looked his surprise at the presence of Blaine.

"A Caldor," said the agent. He looked at Dumarest. "I thought you had more sense."

"Blaine is all right."

"I agree," said the agent. "But, in the dark, who can see the face above the tunic? I get him this room," he said to Blaine. "One from which it is easy to escape. I warn him to see no one. Yet, when I arrive, he is entertaining someone who could be an enemy. How is your cousin?"

"Nursing dreams of vengeance," said Blaine. "Dumarest should have killed him."

"Yes," said the agent. "He should. I am surprised a man of his experience would leave a wounded enemy to do him later harm. On the other hand," he mused, "Ustar would be happier dead. It will be a long time before he is allowed to forget his display of cowardice. Those who wear the dagger are precise about such things."

"You talk too much." Dumarest reached for the parcel the agent carried. "What do I owe you for this?"

"Call it a farewell gift." Yamay watched as Dumarest opened the parcel. The soft sheen of steel-gray plastie rippled in his hands. The scuffed material of his spun-metal clothing had been recovered so that it looked like new. "I have arranged passage for you. To Argentis. Traveling Low."

"Good enough." Dumarest changed, wrapping his discarded clothing in the paper which had held his own. "I will sign an authority before I leave. If you can recover the rest of the money I loaned to Derai it's yours. Blaine here could see that you get it."

"I have already made out the document," said the agent blandly. "I am," he reminded, "a businessman and I was sure that you wouldn't object. If you will sign?"

"Later. When do I leave?"

"In two hours." Yamay looked out of the window. "It would, perhaps, be best not to linger. Ustar may still have a few companions seeking his favor. A little money to the handler will ensure your welcome." He turned, holding out his hand. "Goodbye, Dumarest."

They touched palms.

"Now wait a minute!" Blaine stepped before Dumarest as he turned toward the door. "You can't go like this! What about Derai?"

Dumarest stood, waiting.

"She loves you," said Blaine desperately. "She needs you. You can't let her down."

"You are young," said the agent quickly. "You don't realize what you ask. If Dumarest lingers on Hive he will be killed. Is that what your half-sister would want?"

"No, but—"

"What is your alternative?" Yamay glanced at Dumarest. "There is something I do not know," he said. "We yet have time. Tell me." He listened as Blaine spoke, then slowly shook his head. "Folgone," he said. "I have heard of that place."

"Is what the cyber said true?"

"True enough. And he is right," the agent told Dumarest. "You are needed. In fact, you are essential to their plan. May I negotiate a satisfactory settlement?"

"No," said Dumarest. "It won't be necessary. I know too much about the planet to want to go there. Argentis will do as well."

"Please!" Blaine reached out and touched Dumarest on the arm. "I don't know how to say this. To you it may seem foolish but—" He drew Dumarest to the window and pointed to the stars. "I see them every night," he said. "I meet people like yourself who have traveled among them. There are countless worlds and things to see out there. I'll live and die on this insignificant ball of mud. And every night I'll see the stars and think of what I've missed. This is my chance," he said. "The chance to get out and see something of the universe. You've seen it. Are you going to stop me from doing the same?"

Dumarest looked at the face, no longer cynical, somehow very young.

"At what age," said Blaine, "did you start your travels?"

"I was ten," said Dumarest harshly. "I was alone and more than a little desperate. I stowed away on a ship and had more luck than I deserved. The captain was old and had no son. He should have evicted me but he didn't. I have been traveling ever since."

Traveling, he thought. Going deeper and deeper into the inhabited worlds, leaping from star to star and, because stars were closest away from his home planet, moving always away from Earth. Further and further until even the legend was forgotten and the very name became a joke.

"Ten," said Blaine. "And how old are you now?"

It was a question impossible to answer. Time stopped when traveling Low; slowed almost to a standstill when traveling High. Chronologically he had to be very old; biologically he was not. But, next to Blaine, he felt the age of experience, the only system of reckoning which had any real value.

"You will change your mind," said Yamay. The Hausi was wise in the way of men. "Am I not right?"

"Yes," said Dumarest heavily. "You are right."

Details were basically simple and the agent would attend to all but one. "The sale of the jelly can be none of my concern," he said. "It is not a question of morals, you understand, but of survival. If news of the transaction leaks out I must be free of any suspicion. You must deal with Scuto Dakarti yourself."

The trader had no compunctions. He wanted ambrosaira and didn't really mind where it came from. With no settled interest in Hive he could live up to what he claimed to be. He listened to what Dumarest had to say, pursed his lips as quantities were mentioned, poured wine to settle the bargain.

"I will transfer monies to the Hausi as soon as I have taken possession of the jelly," he said, and almost immediately corrected himself: "When it is safe on board my ship," he added after tasting the wine. "You will understand the precaution?"

"Yes, but time is important. Your ship is on the field?"

"It is. If it were not for the fact that I hope to increase my store I would be tempted to offer it for charter. Perhaps I will. Folgone would offer a ready market for what I would have to sell."

"Extended life," said Dumarest. He was young enough to be able to regard the prospect with impersonal detachment. "From what I've heard, consistent use of the jelly can result in unpleasant effects."

"That is true." Scuto Dakarti lifted the bottle and waited for Dumarest to drink before giving him more wine. "But if you were old and lusted for life would that consideration dissuade you from its use? Believe me, my friend, those who go to Folgone are desperate enough to try any remedy. The more so those who fail to gain a place."

Dumarest frowned; the other was talking of things he knew nothing about. "Place? Are not all welcome on the planet?"

"Yes, but not all can be catered for. You will learn of the difficulties during the journey. You will have time and to spare." The trader sipped at his wine. "I know of the situation," he said. "It is intriguing. The old man

who is the prime Caldor and who must be obeyed. The
family who regard it as their duty to obey. The girl
whom you love and who, so it is said, loves you. The
two brothers." He drained his glass. "You have, of
course, recognized the ramifications?"

"I have been hired to do a job," said Dumarest. "I
am doing it. This is a part of it; the rest I shall do on
Folgone. The pay," he added, "is generous."

"It may be more generous than you guess," said
Dakarti. "If you win a place for the old man he will be
declared legally dead. The succession of the House of
Caldor will fall to Johan, the girl's father. He would,
because of the love he bears for his daughter, undoubt-
edly permit her to marry the man of her choice. You
seem to be that man. Given enough time, my friend,
you could be the actual Head of the House of Caldor.
The owner," he added, "of the eleventh part of the
planet Hive."

"I hadn't thought of that," admitted Dumarest.

"You should. It would be quite an achievement for
any man. The more so for someone who has nothing but
his natural strength and wits to aid him. More wine?"

Dumarest wondered if the man was trying to get him
drunk. If so he would need something stronger than
wine.

"You see now why I feel personally involved," said
Dakarti. "As the potential owner of a fair-sized section
of this world you would be in a unique position. You are
unhampered by tradition. You would be willing to
violate their stupid Pact if, by doing so, you could gain
the advantage. And you would not lack for friends to
see that you gained exactly that. You would, with a
little luck, end by owning the entire planet. You would
have the monopoly of ambrosaira. Can you even begin
to imagine just what that would mean?"

Wealth, of course, and with it power, the two things most likely to appeal to any man. And the trader was right. Both could lie within the hollow of his hand. All he had to do was to win a place on Folgone and marry a girl. No, not just a girl, nothing as simple as that. Marry a telepath. There was a difference. Marry a telepath and forget Earth.

Perhaps, with a woman like Derai, he would be able to do that.

X

FOLGONE was a bleak place, a world of ice and frozen gases, the single planet of a white dwarf star. The surface was sterile; what life existed was buried deep in gigantic caverns lit and warmed by radioactive elements . . . a sealed prison of a world from which there could be no unauthorized escape.

"I don't like this." Blaine wrinkled his nose as they stepped from the drop-shaft which had carried them miles down from the air lock above. "The air smells bad."

Dumarest made no comment. He eased the weight from his arms and shoulders. He and Blaine supported the cocooned bulk of the Old Man and it was both heavy and awkward. To one side Emil conferred with the cyber. Derai, alone, stood immobile. Before he could speak to her the guide Emil had engaged claimed their attention.

"This way, if you please." Carlin gestured to where sheeted plastic stood in walls ten feet high. "Yonder is your accommodation. Snug, private, a place to rest. A moment and we shall be there."

It took ten minutes and Dumarest was sweating by the time they arrived. It wasn't just because of the weight of his burden; the air was warm with a sultry heat, moist with disturbing odors. Inwardly he agreed with Blaine. It smelled bad, nasty, heavy with the taint of rot and decay.

Rid of his burden he looked around. The walls of
plastic stretched to one side, almost filling the horn of a
crescent. Rows of close-set tents filled the other, the far
tip about a mile distant. Opposite the drop-shaft, form-
ing the inner wall of the crescent, stood a wall of stone
thirty feet high. It was topped with fangs of out-curving
steel. Wide doors, now closed, offered the only visible
passage through the barrier.

"That is the near gate," said Carlin. He was young,
intent, eager to display his knowledge. He was not a
native of the planet—none of the guides were. The true
natives chose to remain unseen. "It opens only at the
time of entry."

"Is that when the competitors go in?"

"Yes. The successful aspirants are conducted to the
center by a different route."

Dumarest nodded, looking upward. Overhead the
roof arched up and out in a tremendous sweep, a luminous haze vanishing into the distance. The cavern must
be stupendous. Blaine spoke his question.

"This place—" He gestured to the area in which
they stood. "Why is it so small?"

"It is large enough and filled only at times like this,"
explained the guide. "There are amusements," he
added. "A carnival occupies the far end and, of course,
food and refreshments may be obtained from the com-
missary. Would you like me to get you something?
Wine, perhaps?"

"Yes," said Blaine.

"I'll get it." Dumarest wanted the chance to look
around. "Just tell me where it is."

He heard voices when he returned bearing bottles.
The chambers of the maze-like structure were roofless,
offering visual privacy and little else. Quietly he entered and set down his burden. Derai, he noted, was

absent and so was Regor. They were probably attending the Old Man.

"I was explaining the system by which places are allocated," said Carlin to Dumarest. "Shall I continue?"

"Go ahead."

"As I was saying, there are only so many places available each session," said the guide. "But there are many to fill them. Too many. There has to be some method of determining who shall succeed and who shall fail."

"They could draw lots," suggested Blaine. He reached for one of the bottles of wine. "Or they could auction them to the highest bidder."

"They could," admitted Carlin. "But they don't. The Guardians allow all who have the necessary fee to enter the competition. Some aspirants, of course, enter more than one contender. I have known one man to enter as many as a score."

"And if they win?" Emil was interested. "If they all earn themselves a place?"

"They would receive all the places that were available in the order of their appearance at the far gate."

"So it is possible for one man to win, by proxy, all the places available in any one session?"

"That is so."

Blaine was quick to see the obvious. "Then one man, if he were rich enough, could employ others to compete for him. They would win all the places which he could then auction off at a profit. How about that, Earl? Shall we go into business?"

Dumarest didn't answer.

"You then, Uncle." Blaine was enthusiastic. "You love money and here is a chance to make some. You could return with a hundred fully trained fighting men and really clean up.'' He looked at the guide. ''Are there regulations against anyone doing that?''

''No. But if you hope to corner the market there are difficulties attending such a plan. For one thing, the expense would be vast. For another you would still have no certainty of winning even a single place. The competition isn't only a matter of numerical strength.''

Emil cleared his throat. ''What is it, then? How can a man hope to improve his chances?''

''By having more than one contender working on his behalf.''

''Aside from that?''

''I don't know,'' admitted the guide. ''None but a successful contender could know. You understand the rules?'' He paused, waiting, continuing when he received no reply. ''They are very simple. The contenders enter the operational zone at the near gate. Those who cross the zone and reach the far gate are deemed to be the winners. As many men as there are places available are permitted to pass through. The gate is then closed.''

''And the others? The losers? The ones who arrive late?'' Blaine guessed the answer. ''They die,'' he said. ''They are left to starve.''

He did not see Derai as she entered the chamber to stand behind Dumarest, one hand resting on his shoulder.

''That is so.'' Carlin was somber. ''Now you can see why it takes a man of rare courage to attempt to win a place. Always the odds are against him. It is not enough for him to win. He has to be among the first to do so. If not he loses his life.''

''Earl!''

He felt the hand grip his shoulder, the fingers dig toward the bone, sensed the fear which enveloped her

like a cloak. He lifted his hand to grasp her own. With
the other he reached for wine.

"If the odds are long," he said calmly, "we must
shorten them. Let us drink to that."

He felt her relax as the wine laved his throat.

The soil was dark like granulated coal or charcoal,
full of minerals but devoid of humus, seeming more
like crushed and treated stone than the natural deposit of
forest and fern. Blaine stooped, picked up a handful, let
it trickle through his fingers. The luminescence from
the roof was all about him, killing shadows, distorting
distances. "Are you sure?" he said, not looking at
Dumarest. "Are you certain that you want to go
through with it?"

"Have I any choice?"

"I think you have." Blaine straightened, dusting
black granules from his hand. "You're not of Caldor,"
he said. "You owe us no loyalty. A calculated risk for
pay is one thing but this is different." His voice was
heavy, serious. What Carlin had told them rankled in
his mind. "And there is Derai," he added. "She needs
you. You don't have to do this thing."

"Who then?" asked Dumarest. "You?"

"It is my place."

"Perhaps." Dumarest looked around. They stood
outside the chambers of sheeted plastic facing the open
ground before the gate. Men exercised there. He
pointed toward them. "There are some of your oppo-
nents. Look at them. Could you face any one of them
and hope to live?" He didn't wait for an answer. "They
are your real danger, Blaine. What lies behind that wall
could be bad enough, but nothing in this universe is as
dangerous as men determined to survive. To do so they

would cheerfully kill you. Are you equipped to face
such danger?''

"I could try," said Blaine. A flush stained his
cheeks. "Damn it, I could try!"

"You could," agreed Dumarest. "You could try and
you would fail, so what is the point of trying at all? A
wise man recognizes his limitations. Be wise, Blaine.
And live!''

"And you?"

"I'm stubborn," said Dumarest. "And greedy. I'm
getting paid for this, don't forget. And I intend living to
enjoy my fee." He turned as Derai emerged from the
sheeted plastic. In the light her hair was an aureole of
silver. Her eyes were shadows against the whiteness of
her face. Her hand was cold as she slipped it into his
own, as cold as the surface of the world of Folgone.

"You have a plan," she told him. "You know of a
way to increase your chances. You did not lie."

There had been no need for that; the truth was simple
enough. Men have always gambled on any issue of
which there is doubt as to the outcome, and gamblers
have always tried to adjust the odds in their favor. Men
who have gained experience are always ready to cash in
on it. It was merely necessary to find them. Dumarest
had little doubt as to where that would be.

The carnival was like all carnivals, cramped into
limited quarters but all the more exciting because of
that. Voices called as they walked between the tented
concessions, offering, wheedling, persuading, doing
their best to extract money from one pocket and put it
into another—their own. Offering a moment of tinseled
fantasy in exchange.

"Tell yer fortune, dearie!" A withered crone sat on a
stool before a tent adorned with stellar symbols.

"Learn the future and save yourself heartbreak." She leered at Dumarest. "Discover the secrets of a woman's heart."

"Three tries! Hit once and the prize is yours!" A girl waved a blowpipe, turning to others as they passed.

"You, sir!" A man called to Blaine. "You don't wear that dagger for fun. Ten to one our man draws first blood!"

"Secrets of the competition!" bawled a man. "Learn what lies behind the wall! All the fun of the contest and none of the risk!"

Dumarest hesitated, looking at the man. He was short, scarred, thick of body.

"He lies," whispered Derai. "He knows nothing."

They walked on.

Walked the entire length of the midway and back down a second path, halting when a woman ran forward and threw her arms around Dumarest.

"Earl!" She hugged him tighter, closer. "It's good to see you. Did you come looking for me?"

"Nada." He stepped back, breaking her hold, surprised to see her. Yet there was no cause for surprise. There had been time during the long journey to Hive, the longer one to Folgone, for the carnival to have traveled on its circuit. To him it had been only a matter of days. To her it would have been weeks or months. "How's Aiken?"

"Dead." She looked at Derai, at Blaine, at Derai again. "He had to travel Low and he didn't make it. In a way," she said pointedly, "you killed him. If you hadn't left us he would still be alive."

"I doubt it," he said dryly. He introduced the woman to his companions. Derai said nothing. Blaine was impressed.

"You work at the carnival?" he asked politely.

"There." She jerked her head to where a man stood before a tent. He juggled knives, sending them in a glittering stream high into the air, deftly catching their hilts as they fell. "He's good," she said. "He can throw a blade and split a twig at twenty paces. Better than you, Earl."

"He's had more practice." Dumarest looked at the man. He was dark, young, swarthily handsome. He smiled with a flash of white teeth and let the knives thud into a board at his feet. He jumped forward and held out his hand.

"Jacko," he said. "I've heard of you. Maybe we could get together some time?"

"Maybe," said Dumarest. "In the meantime I'm looking for someone who has won the competition. Not," he emphasized, "someone who knows someone. Or someone who claims to have done it. I want a person who really has. Do you know where I could find him?"

"Why?" Nada's eyes widened as she looked at Dumarest. "You're a contender," she accused.

He nodded.

"You fool!" she said. "You stupid fool!" She looked at Derai. "Did you put him up to this?"

"It's my own idea," said Dumarest impatiently. "Do you know the man I want or don't you?"

"I know him," she said. "But he's going to tell you something you won't like to hear. He's going to tell you that you haven't a hope in hell of getting through that competition alive!"

His name was Lucian Notto. He was a man of middle age, tall, thin, with deep-set eyes and a nervous mannerism of chewing at his bottom lip. He entered the tent and looked around like a furtive animal, relaxing only

when Nada made introductions. He sat at the small
table as she left and helped himself to wine. The neck of
the bottle rattled against the rim of the glass as he
poured.

"I have to be careful," he said. "You can surely
understand that."

"Why?" Dumarest was curt. "You have information," he pointed out. "You are willing to sell it. I am
willing to buy. What is so dangerous about that?"

Notto drank and refilled his glass. The light coming
through the translucent fabric of the tent gave his face a
gaunt, ghostly appearance. Nada's perfume lingering
in the air added to the inconsistency. Outside, Blaine
and Jacko stood guard. The three in the tent sat in an
isolated segment of space—a fit place for the divulging
of secrets.

"You are young," said Notto, looking at his wine.
"And impatient. And," he added, "perhaps even a
little naïve. Do you honestly believe that the natives of
this place would like me to tell you all I know?"

"What they like doesn't matter," said Dumarest
harshly. "What you can tell me does." He reached out
his hand. Derai took it and closed her fingers around his
own. "I want nothing but the truth," he warned. "And
I shall know what it is. If you intend to lie leave now."

"And if I stay?"

"I will pay you," said Dumarest. "Now, to begin,
have you really won the competition?"

"I have."

Dumarest waited for the slight pressure against his
fingers. None came. The man was telling the truth.

"Tell me about it," He reached out and removed the
bottle of wine from Notto's reach. "Later," he promised. "When our business is done. Now talk!"

He sat back, listening, feeling Derai's hand limp

against his own. The system appeared to be simple enough. At a set time the near gate was opened. It stayed open as the contenders passed through. Inside they drew lots for position against the inner wall. Some came early in the hope of drawing a favored place. Others came later, almost at the very last, trusting that others had drawn the unfavorable positions. Finally the gate was shut and the signal given. From then it was every man for himself.

"These positions," said Dumarest. "How do you know which are good and which are bad?"

"You get a map," said Notto. "Inside it's something like a maze. Some routes are easy, others hard. A good start lets you pick your route."

"Can't others follow?"

"They could but it wouldn't be wise. The area isn't barren. Something might miss the first man to pass but it wouldn't fail to get the second."

"Things?" Dumarest frowned. "Such as?"

"Traps, snares, things that sting and claw, creatures of one kind or another. Your guess is as good as mine."

"Don't you know?"

"I didn't meet any of them," confessed Notto. "I was one of the lucky ones. I drew a good position and followed it. There were a couple of tough spots," he recollected, "but nothing an alert and agile man couldn't dodge."

"The map," said Dumarest. "It ended at the far gate?"

Notto nodded. He watched as Dumarest picked up the bottle and spilled wine on the table. With a wet finger he traced lines, the beginnings of a map. "Finish it," he ordered.

"But I told you, you get a map!"

"Of the operational zone, maybe, but I'm not interested in that.'' Dumarest pointed to what he had drawn. "Finish it.''

Notto frowned, drew, hesitated, then drew again. "That's the best I can do," he said. "All I can remember.''

The operational zone appeared to be a flattened ovoid with the gates almost facing each other across the short axis. Beyond the far gate was an indefinite area. Dumarest pointed to it. "What lies there?''

"The center. Where they take the aspirants. Beyond that lies something else. I didn't get a close look at it but it seemed to be a mass of plants. Something like a forest," explained Notto. "A forest of short trees bearing great pods about twelve feet long.''

"After you'd won what happened?'' Dumarest frowned at the map. "How did you get back?'' he demanded. "There must be another route to the center," he pointed out. "Can you remember it?''

"No. I was taken through a maze of passages and sent up a shaft." Notto chewed his bottom lip. "That's all I can tell you.''

It wasn't enough. Irritably Dumarest wiped his hand across the table, destroying the map. "What about weapons?''

Notto shook his head. "You go in empty-handed.'' He leaned over and picked up the bottle of wine. Dumarest leaned forward and tore it from his hands.

"All right," he said tightly. "You've had your fun. Now let's get down to some real facts. As yet you've told me nothing worth paying for. If I'm going to risk my neck I want to know exactly what I'm up against. I want to know how to win. If you have to get paid that's just what you're going to tell me. Now talk," he snapped. "Or I'll give you back the bottle—right smack down the throat!''

Notto gulped, shaking, sweat beading his forehead.
"I—" he gasped. "I—don't look at me like that!"

"I want the truth," said Dumarest. "All of it. Why
did Nada say that I hadn't a chance of getting through?"

"Because you don't," said Notto. He dabbed at his
face with a soiled handkerchief. "No one does unless
he's lucky. It's fixed," he said quickly. "Don't you get
it? It's fixed. The winners are determined at the time of
the initial draw!"

XI

HE WOKE, hearing screams, rolling from his cot and standing all in one quick motion. They came again and he ran, bumping into something hard, ripping plastic to force an opening. Blaine stared at him, dagger naked in his hands, his face shocked.

"Derai!"

The screams came a third time and then Dumarest was in her chamber, kneeling beside her cot, voice soothing as he enveloped her with protective tenderness. Childlike, she clung to him, trembling.

"Derai!" Blaine looked into the room. Quickly he searched with his eyes. "Are you all right?"

"A nightmare." Dumarest spoke over his shoulder. "She's all right now."

"Are you sure?"

"I'm sure."

Blaine hesitated, looking at his dagger. Against terrors of the mind the weapon was useless. Impatiently he thrust it into his scabbard. Neither it nor he was needed at this time.

"Earl!" Her fingernails dug into the back of his neck. "Earl!"

"Be calm now," he soothed. "You had a bad dream. That's all it was."

She shook her head, "It was horrible! I saw endless

rows of naked brains resting in some kind of container, all thinking, all alive and aware. I heard voices and then the universe seemed to open and I became one with all intelligent creatures." Her trembling increased. "Earl, am I going insane?"

"You were dreaming," he said again. "A nightmare."

"No. Not that." She withdrew a little, her eyes on his face. Hungry eyes, desperate, drinking in the sight of his features. "It was so real," she said. "As if my mind was that of another. As if I were completely in tune with another's brain. Someone who was completely relaxed. Relaxed and concentrating on one thing only. Few people can do that," she said. "Always there is noise and confusion. But this was a trained mind. And clear. So very clear."

He said nothing, stroking the silver wonder of her hair, his body responding to the nearness of her own.

"It was like Regor's brain," she said. "He must have a mind like that. Trained, coldly logical, an efficient instrument to use for mental achievement."

"You envy him?"

"No," she said. "He frightens me. He regards me as property. As something to be used. Not as a woman," she added. "He cannot feel that. But as someone important who mustn't be wasted."

"In that we think alike," said Dumarest.

She snuggled against his chest. "That woman," she said. "The one you called Nada. She loves you."

"No."

"She does," Derai insisted. "I know. She loves you and is jealous of me. Jealous!" The word was a cry of pain. "Of what? A freak!"

"Stop it!"

"Why should I? It's true, isn't it? That's what they all think about me. Ustar and Emil and even my father at times. Someone unusual. Someone different. Someone with whom it is impossible to be comfortable. Can you be comfortable when you're with me?" Her eyes held his own, searching, probing. "Can you?"

"I love you."

"Is that an answer, Earl?"

"It should be. The way I regard love it is. What more can I say?"

"Nothing," she said. "But just keep saying it. I like to hear you do that."

He obeyed, stroking her hair, hand tight against her thin shoulders.

She sighed. "That woman," she said. "Nada. She could give you so much. Sons, a normal life, company which would be welcomed anywhere. You would be happy with her. You could relax and think your own thoughts and never had to wonder if, at any moment, she was reading your mind. Why aren't you in love with her, Earl?"

"Because I am in love with you."

"Really, Earl?"

He moved his hands, gripping her shoulders, moving her so that he could stare into her face. "Listen," he said harshly. "This isn't a game. Not for me it isn't, and I hope not for you. Read my mind," he ordered. "Read it and find the truth. Find it and stop playing the child."

"Stop feeling sorry for myself," she said quietly. "Stop doubting everyone I meet. Stop wondering if it's me you love or what I may bring you. Money, Earl. A lot of money. Surely you must have thought of that?"

He looked at her, his face like stone.

"You have thought of it, Earl," she insisted. "Can you deny it?"

"No." Dakarti had planted the thought; he could not deny it.

"Well, Earl?"

He rose, conscious of the futility of words, knowing there was nothing he could say and only one thing he could do.

Alone she wept for a long time into her pillow.

The walls were of garish colors, red, green, yellow, blue, ten foot squares of plastic open to the roof above. Bright hues, the colors of life buried here in this underground cavern, mocking the still figure in the center of the room.

On his stretcher, as if on a catafalque, the Old Man lay dead.

"When?" Regor stood against the wall of red, his robe merging with the background so that he looked little more than a shaved head, a living picture without a frame. He moved on and the illusion was broken, the scarlet of his robe now standing sharp and clear against a background of yellow.

"I don't know." Emil burned with nervous tension. He paced the limited confines of the chamber, unable to remain still. "I was busy," he said. "Settling the details and fees of the competition. When I returned I came in here. At once I sensed that something was wrong. I checked. Nothing. No pulse, no respiration, no sign of life. I tried to find you," he accused. "You were not to be found."

"I was otherwise engaged." Deftly the cyber examined the grotesque bulk on the stretcher. "Has the girl made certain?"

"I asked, she refused. But I heard her screaming some time ago. Blaine said that she'd had a nightmare. It could have been that or she could have caught his dying thoughts." Emil paused in his pacing and stared at the dead man. "Dead," he said bitterly. "And he told us nothing."

Regor made no comment.

"All that money," said Emil. "Fifteen years of income. Gone!"

"You have lost nothing," reminded the cyber.

"Are you insane?" Emil glared at Regor. "You know how I depended on that money. You know what I would have done with it. He could have told us where it was. He could have told us before we left Hive. Instead he kept his secret. Now he is dead and has taken it with him." He resumed his pacing. "And you tell me that I've lost nothing!"

"That is correct," said Regor in his even monotone. "You cannot lose what you have never had to lose. Be logical, not emotional. To accept a probability as an established fact is wrong. A promise is nothing more than that. Until the money was actually in your possession it was never yours. As it was not yours you could never lose it."

"And what of the money I've spent?" snapped Emil. "The cost of the journey here? The expense of the competition? Money that we can ill afford. Gone. All gone. And for what? A dead man's selfishness!" He halted and glared at the corpse as if willing it back to life. "I was too easy," he gritted. "Too soft. I should have made him speak. Forced the secret from him. Killed him to get it if I had to. What could I have lost?"

"Is everything wholly lost?"

"What do you mean?" Emil looked sharply at the cyber. His eyes kindled with hope. "Derai," he said.

"Perhaps she knows? Perhaps he told her, even toward the very last. I can make her tell." He stepped toward the opening, then halted as Regor barred his way. "What now?"

"The girl must not be harmed," said the cyber. His voice was as even as always, a statement of fact, not desire.

"But—"

"She must not be harmed."

Emil surrendered. "What else?"

"Let us consider the position," said Regor. He glanced down at the dead man. He could feel no regret, no sorrow. Even if he could he would have felt neither. The Old Man had served his purpose. "Our initial reason for coming to Folgone is now invalidated," he continued. "What is left? Dumarest is to enter the competition. The fee has been paid and will not be returned. We stand to lose nothing by allowing him to compete as originally intended. He could even win."

Emil nodded, his eyes thoughtful. "The Old Man is dead," he mused. "His place will be vacant. If Dumarest wins we can offer it for sale. Such places command a high price and we could recoup much of what has been spent. But if he does not win?"

He dies, he thought. That too was satisfactory. *It will get him out of the way*, he told himself. *Get rid of him once and for all. Derai would have no one then for whom to yearn. She could blame no one. Ustar would be avenged and the way would be clear for him to marry the girl.* Emil felt himself relax.

Either way he couldn't lose.

"Drink this," said Nada. "Get it all down."

She stood by the side of the cot as she offered the foaming glass. Dumarest looked up at her, smelling her

perfume, conscious of her femininity. She wore a
diaphanous robe tight against the contours of her body.
Her long, dark hair swung loosely over her shoulders.
Heavy makeup gave her face the impassive serenity of
an Egyptian goddess. This was her working costume,
eye-catching as she stood against a wooden backdrop
facing Jacko and his knives. The thrown blades would
cut the fastenings, freeing the garment, finally leaving
her naked in the focused glare of lights.

"Come on," she snapped impatiently. "Drink it!"

He rose on one elbow and obediently gulped the
liquid.

"I've never seen you drunk before," she com-
mented. "Not cold, mean, fighting drunk. You almost
wrecked the midway. Ruined it, anyway. You took on
three men at once," she added. "Bare-handed. They
thought one of them was dead. The other two weren't
much better. The odds were thirty to one against you."

He swung his booted feet over the edge of the cot and
sat upright. He had used her bed. The tent was filled
with her presence, clothes, trinkets, little mementos.
He ran his fingers through his tousled hair. His tongue
felt thick, coated, unclean.

"Can you remember?" She put down the glass he
handed to her.

"Yes."

"So you weren't that drunk then. I'm glad to hear
it." She sat beside him on the cot, pressing close so that
he could feel the long curve of her thigh, the sultry
warmth of her body. "What happened, Earl? Did she
give you the brush off?"

He didn't answer.

"I thought you had more sense," she continued
dispassionately. "A milksop like that. A lady. A

spoiled bitch out to have herself a little fun. And you fell for it. You!''

"Shut up!''

"Why? Can't you bear to hear the truth? Is your ego so hurt? Get wise to yourself, Earl. She isn't our kind of people. What future could you have hoped to have with her?''

She pressed herself even closer, letting her body appeal to his, using the femininity she knew she possessed to work its ancient magic. That, and more.

"You remember?'' she whispered. "When you came here. What you said and what you did?''

There had been a time of lights and noise and bloody action. There had been pain and the desire to fight that pain, to fight it in the best way he knew how. And after? Nada and her tent and a bottle of wine. Wine and—? He tasted the coating of his tongue.

"You drugged me,'' he said. "Slipped something into my drink. Something to knock me out.''

She didn't deny it. "What else could I have done? Let you go and get yourself killed? You were near-crazy, Earl. I had to save you from yourself.''

"How long?'' He rose and looked through the flap of the tent. The midway was deserted. "How long have I been lying here?''

"Long enough.'' She was triumphant. "The gate's open,'' she said. "The competition has begun. Most of the contenders are inside. But not you, Earl. You don't have to get yourself killed. Stay here with me and we'll leave together.''

"Using what for money?''

"We'll make out.''

"No.'' He jerked aside the flap and stepped forward. Nada caught his arm.

"Don't be a fool, Earl. You heard what Notto said. You don't stand a chance of getting through alive."

"I've made a bargain," he said tightly. "I'm going to keep it. Later, when I've money, we can decide what to do. Now I've a job to get on with."

"For her?"

"For me," he corrected. "I'm broke. I need cash. This is my chance to get some."

He pulled free and stepped outside the tent. Jacko glanced at him, busy with his knives. He smiled as he played with the glittering steel. Before he could speak a voice shouted from lower down the line: "Earl!"

It was Blaine. He came running, face streaming with perspiration, dagger bouncing on his hip. "Earl! Thank God I've found you!"

"I was here," said Dumarest. "I've been here all the time. You should have asked."

"I did. They denied having seen you." Blaine fought for breath. "It's Derai," he gasped. "She's taken your place in the competition. She's gone into the operational zone."

There was a crowd outside the gate: sightseers, a few contenders holding back for reasons of superstition or calculated advantage, touts selling advice and dubious information, gamblers and those who were just taking bets. Four guards dressed in brown and yellow stood to either side of the gate, laser rifles cradled in their arms. Four others similarly dressed and armed stood just within the portal. A cowled figure, unarmed but with more relevant power, listened as Dumarest spoke.

"Please." He held up a hand to forestall protest. "You must appreciate the position. Once inside the zone no contender is permitted to leave other than by the far gate."

"But she shouldn't be here at all," stormed Dumarest. "She took my place. It should not have been allowed."

"A moment." The monitor studied a sheaf of papers clipped to a board which he carried beneath his arm. "You represent whom?"

"Caldor."

"The contender for Caldor has passed into the zone. The name was given and the fee has been paid. There is nothing more to say on the matter."

"Like hell there isn't!" Dumarest stepped forward. Immediately two of the inner guards raised their weapons.

"Attempt violence and you will be burned," warned the monitor. "Step forward and the same thing will happen. Now please try to be reasonable. We cannot check the credentials of every contender. It is sufficient that they claim to represent an aspirant and that the fee has been paid. It is rare," he added dryly, "that anyone should attempt such an impersonation. There can be no personal profit, you understand. The person concerned must have had a very good reason for taking your place."

The best, thought Dumarest bitterly. Derai had gone to what she had reason to believe was certain death. She had done it to save his life.

"I've got to get in there," he said. "How can it be done?"

"If you have the fee that will be sufficient." The monitor remained calm. "But you must hasten. Soon the gate will be closed. It will not open again until the next session."

Dumarest whirled, found Blaine, caught him by the upper arm.

"I couldn't stop her," said Blaine. "I didn't know

what she intended. I thought she'd come down to the gate to wish you luck or something. Before I knew it she'd passed inside.''

"Never mind that now.'' The past was irredeemable; Dumarest had no time for regret. "Find Emil," he ordered. "Make him give you the price of a fee and bring it back here fast.''

"What do you intend, Earl?''

"I'm going in after her. Now move, damn you!''

He forced his way through the crowd, turned, saw something he hadn't noticed before. Suspended high above the portal was a large, illuminated board. It was divided into sections. Most were alight with a name and a number. Even as he watched a blank section lit.

"Dumar," said a man at his side. "Position fifteen." He sucked at a stylo and made a notation on a card. "That's his three contenders," he mused. "Twelve, eighty-two and fifteen. Eighty-two won't be of much help. I'd say that the odds on Dumar getting a place were about twelve or fourteen to one against." He looked up at Dumarest. "What do you say, friend?''

"Aren't you favoring him a little?''

"Maybe, but I've seen his boys at practice. Take it from me, they're good.''

Dumarest nodded, looking at the board, now understanding its purpose. He found the name Caldor—position five. Above and below the sections were blank. He nudged his informant and asked a question.

"It's the luck of the draw," the man explained. "That's a bad spot, right down near the end of the zone. Now if Caldor had a couple more contenders lined up and they managed to get placed either side then the odds would be different. The three of them could act as a party, understand? As it is I'd offer, say, fifty to one against.''

"The contender's a woman. A girl."

"Is that so?" The man whistled. "Make it two hundred to one. Five if you like. A rank outsider. She hasn't got a chance."

Dumarest moved on, conscious of the passing of time. How much longer would the gate stay open? Where was Blaine? He turned at the sound of his name.

"Earl." It was Nada, Jacko at her side. "Don't be a fool, Earl," she said. "Your problem's solved."

"Derai's inside."

"That's what I meant." She smiled. "Jacko heard what Blaine said. So she's taken your place. Well, that's just too bad—for her."

"Bitch!"

"You expect me to cry over her?" Nada was defiant. "Why the hell should I? What is she to me? Earl, you fool, why tear yourself apart? Why not just play the cards as they fall." She looked into his eyes. "You're stuck," she said bitterly. "You're in love with her. Really in love. Damn you, Earl! Why couldn't it have been me?"

"You've got to play the cards as they fall," he said dully. "Remember?"

"Can we help?" For once Jacko wasn't smiling. "Nada's upset," he explained. "She doesn't mean half of what she's saying. Is there anything we can do?"

"Can you lend me the price of a contender's fee?" Dumarest knew the answer. "Of course you can't. How could you? And why should you, anyway?" He craned his neck looking over the crowd. "What the hell's keeping Blaine?"

"He's gone for money?" Jacko nodded. "Naturally, what else? He can give you that but maybe I can give you a little something he can't. An edge," he explained. "An advantage the others haven't got."

"A knife?"

"That's it. Get to your position and stay there tight against the wall. Keep an eye open for what may fall close by. I'll try to get you a blade. If I'm lucky I'll make it."

"And if you're caught trying?"

"They'll burn me down," said Jacko calmly. "That's the reason for the guards. That's why I won't be caught. Give me a chance but don't grow old waiting."

Dumarest nodded his thanks. Jacko moved away. From somewhere a gong sounded, deep, sonorous, vibrating the air.

"They're getting ready to close the gate," said Nada. Possessively she took his arm. "Never mind, Earl. You tried."

Impatiently he shook himself free. The gong sounded again as he forced his way through the crowd toward the gate. It was like a tremendous portcullis. As the gong sounded a third time the massive panel began to drop to the ground below.

"Earl!" He turned at the sound of his name. "Earl! Where are you?"

"Blaine!" He rose on tiptoe, sprang high into the air, waved. "Blaine! To the gate! The gate, man! Hurry!"

He caught a glimpse of green and silver, an arm upraised, something dark hurtling through the air above the heads of the crowd. He caught it, a bag, felt coins within the material and turned to face the gate.

Already the panel was almost closed. It was falling faster now that it had almost completed its journey. Dumarest dived headfirst toward the remaining space, felt dirt scrape his face, the lower edge of the door brush his back. He rolled clear as the door ground inches deep into the gritty soil and looked up at leveled guns. He threw the bag of money toward the monitor.

"Your fee," he said.

The monitor caught it, checked the contents, nodded his agreement. "You represent?"

"Caldor."

XII

INSIDE the zone the air was hot, fetid, smelling of decay and with a sharp insect-odor reminiscent of Hive. But there would be no bees here. Bees needed flowers and there were no blooms. Dumarest looked up. Behind him the wall swept inward, the upper edge ten feet beyond the lower. The curve and the fringe of spikes made it impossible to climb. The guards now patrolling the top were an added precaution. He wondered if Jacko would succeed in getting him a knife.

Dumarest leaned back against the wall and took stock of the situation. His position was number forty-three—bad, but it could have been a lot worse. Between him and Derai could be thirty-seven contenders, each of whom would take the chance of an easy kill so as to lower the competition. But the signal had already been given; they would be moving, pressing on to the far gate, leaving the positions to join others of their own group or, if alone, making as much distance as they could to get ahead. In these initial minutes thought was more important than action.

He thought briefly of Notto. Perhaps Nada had told the man to lie or perhaps he really believed what he'd said. It didn't matter. Not now. Nothing mattered except staying alive. Dead he would be useless to Derai.

He moved and felt stone rasp his naked skin. He was stripped to shorts and boots—his own clothes would have given him too great an advantage and the monitor had ordered them removed. But they had left him his

144

boots; he was glad of that. He wondered what the girl would be wearing.

Time was passing, too much time. Already she could be dead, already walking into danger. Impatiently he studied the map which had been thrust into his hand. As Notto had said the place was a maze, torn with winding gullies, scarred with deep channels gouged in the soil, thick with places to hid. Prominent landmarks showed the way to the far gate. It stood at the tip of an elongated neck of land. There, he decided grimly, would be the place of greatest danger. Of all the perils to be found in this place men would be the most to be feared.

He heard a shout from beyond the wall, faint, dulled by thick stone. Above, a guard yelled an order. The noise grew louder and something glittered in the air to quiver point first in the loam. Dumarest snatched it as he ran, his hand closing about the hilt of the knife. Jacko had kept his promise. Perhaps he had arranged a distraction to draw the attention of the guard. Perhaps he had died after throwing the weapon. It didn't matter. Dumarest had his advantage.

He raced toward Derai's position, keeping the wall close to his side, eyes alert for any sign of danger. Here it would be improbable but in the zone the price of life was eternal vigilance. He caught a glimpse of white ahead. A man, operating on the same process of reasoning as himself, came loping toward him. He carried a fist-sized stone in each hand. As they drew close he drew back his right arm and flung the stone.

Dumarest caught it, feeling it smack against his left palm, flinging it back in one coordinated motion. It smashed between starting eyes, turning white into red, pulping the nose. The man groaned and sank to his knees. Without breaking stride Dumarest leaped over him and ran on his way.

One down. The man might be dead or merely unconscious but he was slowed and no longer fit. One
down—how many to go?

A hundred at least. More in all probability. Where
the hell was the girl?

Mechanically he'd been counting paces. He'd arrived at the approximate position but the girl wasn't to
be seen. He halted, chest heaving as he sucked air into
his lungs. *Time,* he thought. *Too much time has passed
since the signal. Jacko held me back too long. She
could be anywhere. How to find her?*

He scowled at the map. She would be scared—more
than that, terrified. The entire area was filled with
thoughts of pain and death. She would need to escape,
but how? Run directly into the unknown? Wait, cring-
ing? Follow the wall? He remembered the man he had
struck down, his vicious savagery. Would he have held
his hand because his victim was a girl? But, if dead,
where was her body?

He looked at the knife, an advantage but useless
now. He slipped it into his boot, forcing his brain to
think, to study data and not emotion. An advantage. An
edge. The knife was one but did he have another?

Unless he found it she would surely die.

A cyber could not feel anger. He could not respond to
the gush of adrenalin into the bloodstream, the engorg-
ing of blood vessels, the tightening of muscle. His body
was an efficient instrument maintaining the brain but
that was all. Anger, hate, fear, love, all were in the
realms of the unknown weaknesses from which lesser
men suffered. The strength of a cyber was in the cold,
calm calculating detachment of an uncontaminated intelligence. But if a cyber could know anger then Regor
would surely have known it now.

"You are positive as to what you say?" His even monotone betrayed nothing. His eyes were twin lenses of a robot but, somehow, the atmosphere was charged with tension.

"The girl is actually in the operational zone?"

"Yes," said Blaine.

"You allowed her to enter?"

"I couldn't stop her. I thought she'd gone to see Dumarest. She entered before I guessed what she intended."

"Dumarest!" The cyber paused. "That man. He has followed her?"

"Yes," said Blaine. "I managed to get the entry fee to him in time." He looked at his uncle. "Emil gave it to me. He didn't want to." He added, "I had to persuade him." With a knife at his throat, he thought, and wondered if he would really have carried out his threat to kill the man had he not yielded the cash.

"He was reluctant?"

"Why not?" Emil had thought the matter out. "It is throwing good money after bad. How can the girl possibly hope to survive?"

Already he had discovered the advantages. With Derai dead there would be none of the difficulty in forcing an undesired marriage. Without a natural successor there would be no trouble from jealous relatives. The Old Man was dead. Johan was now the Head of Caldor. After him? Who but Ustar? And Blaine would make the perfect witness as to Emil's own innocence in the matter. He bared his teeth at memory of the blade at his throat. It would not be long before the young man was safely dead.

Footsteps crunched outside the sheeted plastic. Carlin, their guide, entered. He carried garments folded over one arm. "From your contender," he explained.

"The man Dumarest. I leave them in your keeping."

Blaine took the clothes. "What happens now?"

"As Caldor has two contenders and there is a possibility that both might win you are allowed to send two aspirants to the area beyond the far gate. You will be guided." His eyes drifted, touching one after the other. "Which two you must yourselves decide."

"I'll go," said Blaine quickly. "Dumarest will need his clothes. I can attend Grandfather."

"The Old Man is dead," said Regor. "But go as you suggest."

"Dead?" Blaine looked at his uncle. "When?"

"It doesn't matter," said Regor. "Now go where you must wait." Alone he stared at Emil. "You did wrong," he said. "How often have I told you that no harm must come to the girl?"

"It was her own choice."

"Not so," denied the cyber. "The probable course of events was plain from the first. You knew that she had formed an attachment to Dumarest. That attachment caused her to act under emotional pressure. You should never have allowed the situation to develop. The man should have been eliminated long ago."

"Am I to blame for that?"

"Who else? You assumed the authority and therefore you must accept the responsibility. Because of you the girl is in danger of losing her life."

"And that worries you?" Emil looked thoughtfully at the cyber. "It does," he said. "Why? What is your real interest in the girl? The Cyclan wanted her at their college. Something made her run away. Were you instructed to take care of her? If so you have failed. What does the Cyclan do to those in its service who fail? What happens in such a case?"

Regor made no answer.

"I'm beginning to understand," mused Emil. "The way you people work, secretly, always hidden, maneuvering others as you would puppets. Why, Regor? What is it you want on Hive?"

"Nothing."

"Don't lie to me! I demand the truth!"

"You have it. What could interest the Cyclan on your pitiful world? An anachronism of a social structure? The jelly from mutated bees? No, my lord. There is only one thing of real value which your world has produced: the girl Derai."

"And you want her." Emil bared his teeth at the realization of how he had been used. "You've tried all along to get her into your clutches. First the college and, when she escaped from there, something else. Always remembering to appear innocent. Always appearing as dispassionate advisors and nothing more. The Old Man," he said, remembering. "Did he really have money salted away? Or was that another of your tricks?"

"The plan worked," said Regor. "You left Hive with the girl. You took her from the protection of her stronghold."

"So it was a lie," said Emil. "And you killed him before he could betray it. Or perhaps he simply died. No matter. But you have failed, cyber. You still haven't the girl." He crowed in his triumph. "You've failed!"

"No," said Regor evenly. "Not yet. You forget the man Dumarest. And the Cyclan is not without influence on this world. But you—you know too much."

"And I'm going to know more," said Emil. He had a momentary vision of holding the Cyclan in his power, of the money he could demand for his silence. He looked down as Regor reached out and touched his hand. A single drop of blood welled from the broken skin. "What—?"

Death came immediately. Given not for revenge or hate or from reasons of fear. Given only because Emil could no longer be useful and, worse, could now only be a hinderance to the subtle, insidious, widespread power of the Cyclan.

She walked in a nightmare of strange shapes and stranger voices, of soil that sucked at her feet and stones with mouths that snapped at her garments. There were pictures traced in screaming lines of pain: a man, paralyzed, pleading with his mental voice while, about him, spined and hollow vines drank of his blood; another trapped in a pit at the bottom of which giant mandibles snapped in frenzied anticipation. Death and pain and the fear of death washed around her like the waves of a sea. Madness was everywhere.

Only the voice was sane.

"Derai. Derai. Come to me. Dumarest speaking. I'm at the foot of the column of stone. The first landmark to the right of your map. Derai. Derai. Come to me. . . ."

At times the voice wavered. Twice it ceased and red fury had washed where it had been. But always it had returned. Blindly she made toward it.

"Derai!"

Her feet pulled at sucking ooze.

"Derai!"

It was no longer just a mental voice, a repetitious sound in her head, rising by sheer persistence above the other demanding echoes. It was real, made by a tongue and lips, warm flesh and living blood. "Earl!"

She ran forward and felt his arms around her, strong

arms, protecting, shielding her from the horror that was the operational zone.

"Derai!" He held her, stroking her hair, then pushed her back, his eyes anxious as they searched her for injury. "Are you hurt?"

"No."

"Are you sure?" Again he examined her. She wore a simple shift of synthetic fiber tied at the waist with a strand of silk. They had taken her outer clothes and left her with the feminine equivalent of shorts. Her feet were bare; she had lost her sandals. His lips tightened at the sight of blood against the too-white skin. "Did anything sting you? Quick, girl. Answer!"

"Nothing." She was positive of that. "I fell against a bush," she said. "It was covered with thorns. They scratched my legs, my feet." She looked down. "I don't know how I lost my sandals."

"But nothing else?" He held his breath until she shook her head. "Thank God for that!"

His plan had worked. The other thin advantage they possessed had given him the needed edge. To find her had been hopeless—she'd had to find him. Find him by following his mentally shouted directions. He had trusted to her telepathic ability to solve the problem. But it had not been easy.

"Earl!" She looked at his face, drawn from long concentration, the haunting fear that he was wasting his time, that she couldn't hear him, that she was already dead. Blood stained his right arm. Not his own, she realized with a wave of thankfulness; he was unhurt. The red fury she had felt must have been when he'd fought off attack. "It isn't easy," she said, gently touching his face. "To sit and do nothing but think. To concentrate as you did."

"No," he said. "It isn't easy."

"You followed me," she said. "Why?" It was a stupid question. She knew why. "Earl, my darling. I love you. I love you!"

He looked into her eyes.

"And you love me," she said. "I know that. I've known it all the time but—"

"You tried to save me," he said. "I understand. There's no need to talk of it again. But do you still doubt me?"

Her arms, her lips gave him the answer.

"Steady!" They had found each other but that was all. The journey to the far gate had still to be made, lost time had still to be recovered. Somberly he looked at her, more like a silver-haired child than ever in the torn and soiled slip, the bare and scratched feet. Like a child from some industrial slum. It was hard to remember that she was the successor to wealth and power. Too hard. He preferred to think of her as she was at the moment: young, weak, needing his protection.

Needing his strength as he needed her ability.

"We can win," he said. "We can get out of this but we have to do it together. Your mind," he said. "Can you tell distance from what you hear?"

"Sometimes," she admitted. "If a voice is strong then usually it is near. A mind rather—I get confused."

Naturally, there were no words to describe telepathic phenomena. But "voice" would serve.

"You're going to guide me," he told her. "I'm going to carry you on my shoulders. You're to listen for anything like a threat. If you hear something you must tell me at once. Don't bother to make sure about it. If there's danger let me know. Understand?"

Slowly she nodded.

"Can you tell the difference between, say, a vegetable and a man?"

"A vegetable doesn't think," she said. "It—well, just is."

"An insect?"

She shuddered.. "No words. Just a cold ferocity."

"All right," he said, deciding. "Concentrate on men. When you hear one close let me know. Climb up now." He waited as she mounted his shoulders, painfully light, slim thighs to either side of his head. "Settled?"

She gripped his hair. "Yes, Earl."

"Then hang on tight."

Knife in hand he ran toward the distant sanctuary of the far gate.

It was a twin of the other, set in a thirty foot wall of spiked stone, a great portcullis, a guillotine to cut short the lives of men. Above it glowed a great numeral four. Four what? Four had already arrived? Four places yet to go? Dumarest halted, easing the burden in his arms. Haste now could be suicidal. Men could be lurking, waiting for others of their group to join them, killing all others who arrived first.

He shook the girl in his arms. "Derai!"

She lolled, waxen, the bruise on her temple livid against the white skin. His face tightened as he looked at it. A stone flung by an unseen hand had almost killed her. Riding on his shoulders she had made a tempting target and had recognized the danger too late. For the past three hours he had carried her in his arms, running, forced to smell out danger alone.

"Derai!"

She moaned, moving her head a little, a person still unaware. He frowned and looked about, eyes darting, ears strained. Nothing. And that seemed wrong. So close to the gate there should have been the furtive movements of cautious men. There should have been shouts, cries of despair or triumph and, perhaps, the screams of the dying. The silence, the stillness, was unnatural.

He fought the temptation to sit and rest. For what seemed an eternity he had run and halted, dodged and circled, skirted danger and attacked when attack could not be avoided. His body ached and burned with fatigue. His eyes felt full of grit, dusty, unreliable. But they had made good time. Up until the incident of the thrown stone very good time. His hands clenched as he thought about it. The man would throw no more stones. But the need to carry her dead weight since then had slowed him down. The denial of her telepathic cooperation had slowed him even more.

Cautiously he began to advance. Almost at once he halted, realizing how vulnerable he was with the girl in his arms. He set her down, stooped, threw her over one shoulder, clasping her arm with his left hand, his left arm around her legs.

Above the gate the glowing sign suddenly changed to the numeral three.

So the sign showed the number of places left. Dumarest scanned the area once more and knew that the time for caution was over. The time margin was too narrow for that.

He ran, thrusting his feet against the soil, sucking air into his lungs, eyes darting ahead and to all sides. Blood roared in his ears and sweat stung his eyes. Steel fingers clawed at his lungs as his body used oxygen faster than he could take it from the air. Blackness edged his vision. Doggedly he ran on.

He saw the man just in time, jumping over the sprawled shape, running on without breaking stride. A second figure lay slumped to one side. At the third he paused, instinct screaming of hidden danger, conditioned reflex sending him dropping to the dirt.

Nothing. No shout. No sound of an energy weapon. Not even the soft thud of feet or the rasping of air-starved lungs. Only the throb of blood in his head, the burning agony of his chest.

Quickly he examined the man. He was dead without visible cause. His neck was intact, there was no congestion of the throat, no bruising of the flesh. And no cut or stab or burn. He had simply died.

Dumarest felt the crawling of his skin, the primitive warnings of danger. Quickly he picked up the girl and raced toward the gate. The numeral changed as he neared it, the light now showing a great figure two. Before him the path seemed to stretch to infinity, the gate retreating as he ran.

Then he had reached it, was falling through it, hitting the dirt as his knees collapsed, the girl rolling from his shoulder, outraged lungs filling his chest with pain.

Fighting the wave of blackness which threatened to engulf him, he heard the rumble and thud as the door slammed down.

XIII

THERE WERE boots, a brown and yellow robe, a cold face looking down. "You have a knife," accused the monitor. He glanced to where the hilt showed above Dumarest's boot. "Weapons are not permitted in the zone."

"I found it." Dumarest raised his head, climbed painfully to his feet. He had made a mistake. He should have discarded the blade before passing through the gate. The error could be serious. "I found it," he repeated. "I did not enter with it. You know that. You searched me yourself."

"True." The monitor stood, brooding. "There was a disturbance by the near gate," he said. "A man was killed. You could have arranged for him to have thrown you the blade."

"I or another," admitted Dumarest. So Jacko was dead. Well, he had known the risk.

"If you had done so," said the monitor, "you would be disqualified. Burned to death for breaking the rule."

"I found it," insisted Dumarest. His eyes were hard, direct as he stared at the man in brown and yellow. "It was in the zone. Am I to be blamed for using it?"

The monitor hesitated, his eyes straying to the girl. "There is doubt," he admitted. "You may have the benefit of it. But you will not again be welcome on Folgone."

He left and Dumarest watched him go. Tall, arrogant, holding in this place the power of life and death.

He looked around. Facing the gate a crowd of men stood behind a barrier: aspirants gathered to see if they had won a place. A small group were walking from it: those who had been successful. Among them he saw Blaine.

The sound of water echoed to one side. A rivulet cut across the gritty soil, a narrow barrier between him and the vegetation beyond. He picked up the girl and walked toward it, setting her gently down, plunging head, arms and shoulders into the stream. It was ice cold in comparison with the sultry atmosphere. He plunged fully into the water, washing the mud, blood and slime from his body. The chill shock caught his breath, dissolved some of his fatigue. Returning to the girl he carried her to the edge of the stream and gently laved her face, the purple bruise on her temple.

"Earl." She moved, twisting her face from the cold impact, opening her eyes. "Earl!"

He sensed her terror, her unspoken fear. "It's all right," he soothed. "It's all over. We won. We're out of the zone and safe."

She relaxed, reading his mind, knowing that he spoke the truth. Her arms lifted, circled his neck. "Earl," she whispered. "My darling. I love you so much."

He held her, conscious of her elfin beauty, the long, slender lines of her body, the silver wonder of her hair. He felt an unaccustomed peace. Here, in the circle of her arms, was all he had ever wanted, all he could ever want.

Footsteps approached. Blaine stood beside them, looking down. "You won," he said. "I'm glad." He waited as they rose to their feet. "The other winning aspirants have gone into the woods," he said. "We're about the last."

"Into the woods?" Derai frowned. "Why?"

"To claim their places. There's a bridge lower down," said Blaine. "But I guess we can cross here easily enough." He jumped the stream, waited for them to join him. Together they looked at what lay ahead.

It was as Notto had said, a mass of what appeared to be stunted trees, bushy, bearing gigantic pods trailing on the ground, a few open, the rest tightly closed. Dumarest scuffed the dirt with the toe of his boot, stooped, picked up a handful and let it trickle between his fingers. It was rich, dark, thick with humus. A balanced, fertile loam. He looked back at the wall of the operational zone; the logic of the system was now obvious. The contenders did more than provide money; the dead supplied a steady stream of fertilizer.

He looked up at the roof arching high overhead, a shimmer of distant light, then back at the plants. The air held a jungle-scent, a tropic lushness part soft, part acrid. Beside him Derai took his hand.

"I can hear them," she whispered. "But they think so fast! So terribly fast!"

Dumarest closed his fingers on her own. "The plants?"

"No, the people. But they think so fast. Too fast," she complained. "I can't make out detail. It's just endless noise."

Subjective hallucination, he remembered. A year crammed into a day. The closed pods held people, the old, the crippled, the dying; partaking in a symbiotic relationship with the parent plant, providing essential minerals and animal matter in return for a thousand years of endless dreams. The pods—the coveted places of Folgone.

"I don't know if we're doing the right thing," said

Blaine dubiously. "I don't know if we should be here at all. We have no use for a place now," he explained. "The Old Man is dead."

"I know," said Derai simply. "I heard him die."

"Emil too." Blaine frowned as they approached the vegetation. "He was all right when I first left," he said. "I had to go back for something. I found him lying dead. I don't know what killed him."

Dumarest was sharp. "Did you leave him alone?"

"Regor was with him. Why?"

"Where is Regor now?"

"Here," said the cyber evenly. "I am here."

He stood, scarlet against the yellow and brown of the plants, very tall, his face thin, austere against his thrown-back cowl. His hands were buried with the sleeves of his robe. On his breast the Cyclan seal moved a little with the movement of his breathing.

Dumarest released Derai's hand, took three quick steps toward the scarlet figure.

"That is far enough." Regor glanced at the girl. "You look ill," he said evenly. "Why don't you sit down?"

She shook her head but moved a little to one side, edging forward so that she was level with Dumarest. Blaine glared at the cyber, twenty feet distant. "You killed Emil," he accused. "It could have been no one else. Do you deny it?"

"No."

"He doesn't need a reason," said Dumarest harshly. "He and his breed operate on a different system of logic than normal people. Perhaps he was ordered to kill him. Perhaps he did it as you would kill a fly. Why are you here?" he demanded. "What do you want?"

"The girl."

"I thought so." Dumarest remembered the dead men he had found in the zone. "You were protecting us," he said. "Why?"

"The Cyclan has friends on this planet," said Regor evenly. "I gave orders that the girl was to be saved no matter what the cost. You were fortunate," he said. "An accident saved you. Had you not been carrying the girl you too would have died."

"Derai?" Blaine looked baffled. "But why should you go to all that trouble? What is so special about her?"

"She is a telepath," said Dumarest. He didn't look away from the cyber. "She is important to him and to his people."

"More than that." Regor seemed to grow even taller. "How can you guess at her potential worth? You creatures of contaminated intelligence, slaves to hampering emotions, living for the moment instead of the centuries to come. That girl is a telepath. A telepath has power—more than you could ever guess, more than she could ever dream. To know the thought behind the word, the motive behind the thought, to kindle hate and fear and greed at will. To soothe, to be able to lie, to have the ability to tell a person exactly what that person wants to hear. To know someone so well that he has no choice but to act according to your will. A telepath can do that. A telepath can know a man better than he knows himself. Such knowledge is power."

"Power for the Cyclan," said Dumarest. "To give you the one thing you lack: a true knowledge of emotion. And Derai could give it to you."

"No," said Blaine. "You know how she is, Earl. Afraid almost all the time. You have given her security. Without it she will go insane." He looked from Dumarest to the cyber, understanding. "It doesn't matter,'' he said blankly. "You don't really care what happens to her mind. You don't regard it as important.''

"It isn't," said Dumarest tightly. "Not to them."

"No," said Regor. His even monotone made him seem more robotic than before. "Her mind is nothing. We are interested only in what she carries inside her body. Her seed. The genes which bear the genetic pattern of telepathy. Her body to produce young.''

"No," she whispered. "No!''

Regor ignored her. "It may be necessary to operate on her brain,'' he said. "Tranquility will be an important factor in the development of the foetus. The telepathic ability must appear in the very womb.''

"You're forgetting something," said Dumarest. "Derai is the result of a million-to-one chance of successful mutation. To repeat it would require her mother and father both—and her mother is dead.'' He remembered the village. "You," he said. "Your people. The Cyclan raided the village of Lausary and took the inhabitants. Why, cyber? More experimental material for your laboratories?''

"The Cyclan covers every eventuality," said Regor. "The probability of the girl escaping us was small but not to be ignored. Her mother came from Lausary. The conditions which led to her mutation may have similarly affected others. We shall see.''

"Perhaps," said Dumarest tightly. His hand dropped a little, falling toward his knee.

"You killed Emil," said Blaine. He seemed baffled by the enormity of what he had heard. "You raided a village of Hive. Now you calmly talk about stealing Derai. How do you hope to get away with it?''

"Two contenders won two places for Caldor," said Regor. His hand moved a little within his sleeve. "Two places were won and two will be occupied. The girl will simply vanish. No one will think to blame the Cyclan. Why should they? What possible connection could we have with such a matter?''

He was enjoying the only pleasure he could ever know, the knowledge that a prediction was proving correct, the cerebral satisfaction of mental achievement.

''And us?'' Blaine asked the question. ''What about us?''

Derai threw herself forward as Regor took his hand from his sleeve.

Dumarest saw it, heard the sibilance of the laser beam as it vaporized atmospheric moisture, smelled the char, the blood, heard the scream of pain. He caught the girl with his left arm, his right hand flashing to the top of his boot, up, forward, the knife a shimmer of steel as it left his hand. Regor choked, fell to his knees, toppled sidewise, the handle of the blade an ugly protuberance from his throat.

''Derai!'' Dumarest eased her to the ground, looked at what the cyber's weapon had done. ''Derai!''

He knew she was dying.

The beam had cut through the lower abdomen, charring muscle, fat and intestine, cutting almost to the spine. There was little blood since the cauterizing action of the beam had sealed the external wound. But she was dying. Dying!

''Derai!''

She opened her eyes, looked up at him, lifted one hand to touch his face. ''Earl.'' Her fingers lingered on his mouth. ''I read his mind,'' she whispered. ''I knew what he intended. He forgot I could do that.''

Forgot or didn't care or had ignored the possibility of self-sacrifice.

"Derai!" He felt his throat tighten, his eyes sting as if he were again a child. His voice was an echo of pain. "Derai!"

"It doesn't matter, darling," she whispered. "You are alive and that's all that's important. Important to me, dearest. I love you, Earl. I love you."

How could he let her die?

He rose, the girl cradled in his arms, careless of the blood welling from the slashed abdomen. His eyes were wild as he searched the plants. The gleam of an open pod caught his eye and he ran toward it.

"A moment!" A figure in brown and yellow, armed, invisible against the vegetation, moved to bar his path. "What do you intend?"

"This girl has won a place," said Dumarest tightly. "She's going to get it."

"Agreed," said the guard. "But this pod is not yet ripe. Take the one over there." He pointed with his gun. "And remove her garment," he called. "She must be nude."

The pod was big, open, lined with an inches-deep fuzz of flaming scarlet; a countless number of hair-fine hypodermic needles made from the vegetable matter itself. Dumarest tore away the charred, blood-soaked shift, lifted the slender body, laid it gently within the pod. Immediately it reacted, the fuzz pressing hard against the white skin, penetrating it, the edges of the pod beginning to close.

"Derai, my darling." Dumarest stooped over her. "You'll be all right now," he promised. "You'll be happy. Happier than at any other time of your life."

"With you, Earl?"

He nodded. He would be in her dreams as long as she wished him to be there. "I love you," he said abruptly. His hands clenched as he fought his grief. "I love you."

"I know it, my darling." She smiled, sleepily; already the injected drugs had robbed her of pain. "Earl, my darling, remember Earth? You thought I was teasing you but I wasn't. It does exist, dear. Regor knew of it. Regor or some of the others. I forget just who."

"The Cyclan?"

"That's right, darling. At the college."

Dumarest felt the hand on his arm, the tug as the guard tried to pull him back. "You must not impede the process," he warned. "Please step back where you can do no harm."

Dumarest shook off his hand. The pod was almost wholly closed now, the lower edges sealed so that only her face and the silver glory of her hair remained visible. Against the scarlet interior she looked ethereal.

"Good night, Derai," he called softly. "Pleasant dreams."

She smiled, too sleepy, too cozy to answer. As he watched, the edges of the pod closed over her face.

He would never see her again.

Regor lay where he had fallen, the scarlet from his throat merging with the scarlet of his robe, the thick trail of blood almost obliterating the seal on his breast. Blaine hesitated beside the dead man. "Earl?"

"Leave it to rot!" Jacko was dead and wouldn't need his knife. And, for Dumarest, the cyber was a thing of hate.

"I'm sorry, Earl." Blaine fell into step beside him. "About Derai. I'm sorry."

"Don't be sorry for her." Blaine would miss his half-sister. Johan would miss his daughter. Dumarest could spare them grief. "She's happy," he said. "She'll be happy for a thousand years. Her time, not yours, but still a thousand years. She isn't dead," he added. "Don't think that. She has what men would pay high to obtain. What men fight and die trying to get."

A synthetic existence, cocooned in the pod, her body becoming one with the plant which nurtured her brain, supplying it with oxygenated liquids to emulate blood, with drugs so that her hallucinatory dreams were as real as normal life. As real and far more satisfactory for, in the pod, there was no pain, no fear, no disappointment. And no death. No death at all.

Not even at the very end when only the brain remained and, imperceptibly, her intelligence would merge with that of the plant itself. Merge and wait for another to fill a pod when she would share the vicarious experience of a new intelligence.

"I wasn't thinking of Derai," said Blaine awkwardly. "I'm sorry for you, Earl."

"Don't be." The grief was sharp but it would dull. Life had to go on. There would be other worlds, other things to do, action to fill the aching void, the memory of what might have been. "You're alone now," he said to Blaine. "You've got to save what you can. We won two places. Derai took one but you can sell the other. The money should help. It will get you back home and leave plenty over."

"It's yours, Earl."

"I worked for pay. That you can give me. Derai earned the rest."

They walked in silence and then, "What are you going to do now, Earl?" Blaine didn't wait for an answer. "Come back to Hive with me. We'll adopt you into the House. Please, Earl. We need you."

He spoke from emotion, not truth. Blaine would return and Johan would do what he should have done long before. With Emil dead and Ustar in disgrace who else could succeed him but his natural son? The House would accept him as such. And a ruler should not rely on others.

And how could he live in the stronghold which had held Derai? Be a part of her family with its painful associations?

"No," he said sharply. "I go my own way."

"All right." Blaine was disappointed. "You know best. But promise me one thing. If you ever need help call on Caldor. Don't forget us, Earl," he insisted. "Don't do that."

Promises, thought Dumarest. The gratitude of princes. Well, perhaps Blaine was different from the rest. He could mean what he said. But now?

He straightened, feeling the reviving power of anger. The Cyclan had robbed him of the woman he loved. For that it would pay. Until now he had disliked the scarlet-robed cybers for what they represented. Now he had cause for active hate.

And they knew the whereabouts of Earth.

Derai had told him that. She had not lied.

He turned and looked back at the plants, the sealed pods. One of them held the girl in its healing embrace—it was impossible to tell which.

"Goodbye, my darling," he murmured. "Thank you—for everything."

Then he turned.

And looked back no more.

WHY WASTE
YOUR PRECIOUS
PENNIES ON GAS OR
YOUR VALUABLE
TIME ON LINE
AT THE BOOKSTORE?

We will send you, FREE, our 28 page catalogue, filled with a wide range of Ace Science Fiction paperback titles—we've got something for every reader's pleasure.

Here's your chance to add to your personal library, with all the convenience of shopping by mail. There's no need to be without a book to enjoy—request your *free* catalogue today.

ALL TWELVE TITLES AVAILABLE FROM ACE
$2.25 EACH

- [ ] 11630 **CONAN, #1**
- [ ] 11631 **CONAN OF CIMMERIA, #2**
- [ ] 11632 **CONAN THE FREEBOOTER, #3**
- [ ] 11633 **CONAN THE WANDERER, #4**
- [ ] 11634 **CONAN THE ADVENTURER, #5**
- [ ] 11635 **CONAN THE BUCCANEER, #6**
- [ ] 11636 **CONAN THE WARRIOR, #7**
- [ ] 11637 **CONAN THE USURPER, #8**
- [ ] 11638 **CONAN THE CONQUEROR, #9**
- [ ] 11639 **CONAN THE AVENGER, #10**
- [ ] 11640 **CONAN OF AQUILONIA, #11**
- [ ] 11641 **CONAN OF THE ISLES, #12**

Available wherever paperbacks are sold or use this coupon.

ACE SCIENCE FICTION
P.O. Box 400, Kirkwood, N.Y. 13795

Please send me the titles checked above. I enclose $_____
Include $1.00 per copy for postage and handling. Send check or
money order only. New York State residents please add sales tax.

NAME_____

ADDRESS_____

CITY_____STATE_____ZIP_____

A-04

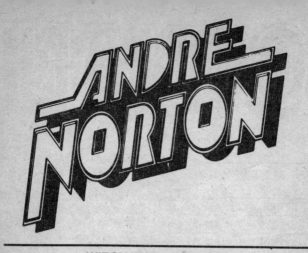

WITCH WORLD SERIES

☐ 89705	**WITCH WORLD** $1.95	
☐ 87875	**WEB OF THE WITCH WORLD** $1.95	
☐ 80806	**THREE AGAINST THE WITCH WORLD** $1.95	
☐ 87323	**WARLOCK OF THE WITCH WORLD** $2.25	
☐ 77556	**SORCERESS OF THE WITCH WORLD** $2.50	
☐ 94255	**YEAR OF THE UNICORN** $2.50	
☐ 82349	**TREY OF SWORDS** $2.25	
☐ 95491	**ZARSTHOR'S BANE** (Illustrated) $2.50